Praise for To Another Abyss!:

"*To Another Abyss!* is a hilarious send-up of the post-post-modern art scene set in the eldritch world of Lovecraft's New England. Bartlett's debut crackles with smart-ass dialogue and lefty politics galore, as well as an unlikely set of characters you'll quickly grow attached to. Fuckin' A!"

– Erica L. Satifka, British Fantasy Award-winning author of *Stay Crazy*

TO ANOTHER ABYSS!

Zach Bartlett

TO ANOTHER ABYSS!

ZACH BARTLETT

SPACEBOY BOOKS

Denver, Colorado

Published in the United States by:
Spaceboy Books LLC
1627 Vine Street
Denver, CO 80206
www.readspaceboy.com

First printed May 2018

ISBN: 978-0-9997862-2-2

TO ANOTHER ABYSS!

Zach Bartlett

To everybody else on the left kicking up dust.

1

When I got to the gallery that morning, I found a manila envelope wedged partway through the mail slot with 'this also not intended for framing' written in place of the return address. Upon removing it, I saw 'YOU PRIG' in place of the mailing address, and knew that I had another Manifestians letter to deal with.

This particular group got it into their heads that modern art (different from Modern art, which means a bunch of Rothkoey squares, though they weren't fond of that either,) was evidence of a culture in decline. They believed it fell upon them to remedy this not by creating better art, but by creating a series of open letters, theses, and manifestos decrying the state of modern (as well as Modern) art and publishing them across every corkboard and lamp post they could find.

They also liked making a big deal out of presenting their manifestos to prominent figures in the Treebridge,

Massachusetts art scene.

When they presented me with one a few months ago, I'd mistaken it for some sort of avant-garde performance-object and had it framed and hung in the gallery. Rather than taking my actions as an insult, which I hadn't intended, they took it as a statement, which I also hadn't intended but was apparently even worse. Not three days after it was hung, one of their number was outside the gallery on his hands and knees, wearing a smock that had "soapbox" printed on it; while another, shorter member stood on his back and accused me of being post-*this* and callously-dismissive-of-*that*, and unlike much of the art scene here, I actually pride myself on being described with as few hyphens as possible. I was just about ready to hand them back their manifesto when the soapbox slipped a disc and they both left the premises, but the group has had it in for me ever since.

Their actual name is an acronym with too many consonants to pronounce, like it's Gaelic or something. I'd originally called them Letterists until a more art-savvy friend told me that term meant something completely separate from what they're doing.

I tucked their envelope beneath my arm, unlocked the door, then used my boot to shove a foot-square ceramic cube which might have been an old exhibit in front of the door to prop it open. It was around eleven o'clock, which was later than I preferred to open on weekdays. But, one advantage I'd noticed to living in a college town was that I was rarely the person running latest in any given situation.

I flicked the lights on and, as I occasionally did when there wasn't anybody else around, briefly indulged in the feeling of standing in a room filled only with art that I thought, for lack of a more studious term, looked wicked cool. At that time, we had one corner showing off some portraits done in swooping inks by a visiting Mount Holyoke lecturer, a tall brass sculpture my friend Myra designed, that looked like a memorial for a battle-worn pencil, and a section of scenic local photographs that were rather popular as postcards. My favorite of the current crop was a geometric line painting, similar to a constellation chart viewed through a fish-eye lens, titled "They Owed Nothing to the Light of Day" by an artist named Donald Verrick. There was a mathematical term I'd heard people use to describe it that I can't recall, but regardless I loved the way the insanely-angled blue lines spiraled across its anguished orange background like a crumpled and gaudy tartan blanket.

After aesthetically reassuring myself, I crossed the main gallery space to my office, which I regarded in much the same manner a cat might regard a full sink it was being carried towards.

I founded the Withers Art & Inspiration Foundation, an offshoot of my folks' own philanthropic trust, in order to begin offering a yearly grant to a local artist so they could afford themselves more time to create local art. Being inexperienced, I took the easy route and given it to my friend Myra, the first year. In my defense she used it to produce some excellent-looking and moderately well selling art. The favoritism, though, left a bit of guilt on the conscience.

This year, I was determined to solicit applications and award the grant in the proper manner, though I'd run into a minor snag the previous day, when none of the applications I'd received seemed particularly artful. The first one I read proposed to create a videogame that "imbued the player's choices with meaning and consequence," the second wanted to leave a bunch of lights on in a house nobody lived in for the next year, and the third planned to build a large purple wall that passersby would be encouraged to write inspirational quotes on with paint markers. That was the point where I gave up for the night and decided to watch the season premiere of

"The Alan Thicke Mysteries" instead.

I sat at my desk, where, against my hopes, the same stacks of applications remained from the night before. I began reading the next application on the pile with a firm sense of duty, but had to stop when I got to the words "created from found objects," and placed it on the discard pile with a sigh.

It's not that I disliked the odd slant-art things which seem to crop up wherever you get young people with free time and enthusiasm gathered in numbers—I made sure to tip human statues and that one street performer with the pedal-powered glockenspiel whenever I walked by—but I'd always thought there should be something more to capital-A Art, than some little gimmick you smile and hand a dollar to while on your way to a restaurant. Treebridge had plenty of those on its street corners any given day who seemed to be supporting themselves just fine on whatever landed in their open instrument cases.

I wondered sometimes if their numbers were simply due to the significant amount of street corners we had, like a nature-abhors-a-vacuum sort of principle. Treebridge, like much of the state, had streets that tended to curl awkwardly around each other, like squid consoling themselves after a night of heavy drinking. It was one part of what Treebridge State University's recruiters call our "modernized, rustic, small-town ambiance," which was a concept the school's left-leaning adjuncts shortened to "Thoreau-fellating WASP porn."

After some time frowning at the applications, I noticed a shadow falling across my office door; a literal one in addition to the metaphorical one that hung over me. My door had a window of textured glass which from inside allowed me to see if there was anybody milling about in the gallery, and from the outside alluded to there being an actual office behind it. This was due to my old door accidentally getting purchased by somebody who mistook it for an installation piece that they said

4

"drew attention to the power of the visual medium through its stark absence." I couldn't bring myself to disappoint him if he really enjoyed the door that much, and his initial offer was enough for me to get a nicer one installed.

So it was through my new window that I noticed someone approaching who soon bellowed: "Tell me I can come in, Greg, it feels like that damn non-Euclidean painting is leering at me."

Like a ray of snide sunlight shouldering its way through heavy clouds, an end to the morning's doldrums had suddenly presented itself in a third party with more articulate taste than my own.

I consented to the demand and Decca barged in to immediately deposit herself in the chair across from my desk, becoming a pile of boots and sweater beneath a shaggy, shortish hairstyle that she kept correcting my names for. She slapped a thick folder full of stapled sheets of paper on to the desk, next to my own similar stacks.

"Were you grading Intro Lit papers all last night too?" she asked after a pause, seemingly having planned a different opening line.

"Worse: the year's grant applications."

"Ah yes, your little noblesse oblige project." She picked up and flipped through the pre-discarded pile. "Wanna place bets on which of our folders' contents displays a better grasp of critical theory?"

"You know I haven't the slightest idea how to determine that."

"Eh, you can cobble together a good proxy argument when you've had a few. Besides, we can read them in dumb voices and laugh."

"I've never hesitated to do that with your assignments, but there's deadlines to be met and stakes to, uh, stoke," I said. "I need to decide which of these applicants to give the grant to, but none of them seem all that artistic to me."

She gave an exaggerated shrug. "Just hand it to Miss BankNorth again."

Myra's slight notoriety after winning the first year's grant got her a commission to make one of those metal, swishy-shaped block statues for their main branch's downtown lobby. She wasn't particularly ashamed of the commercial aspect, though she said she didn't put any real thought in to the piece and just based it on things she'd seen in front of other office buildings. She apparently had a scrapbook of them.

"I don't want the W.A.I.F. to be a complete inner-circle-jerk sort of thing. It should be fair and open to everyone, even if most of them do have bad ideas."

"First, that's refreshingly idealistic of you. Second, aside from the financial backing that's all that the Beats were, and the kids I teach are still drooling over them fifty years after the fact. Despite my best efforts."

I clasped my hands together on the desk before me, hoping to appear more official for what little sway that may have had with her.

"I'm in a bind here. I can't tell whether I'm just being a snoot or whether these things really aren't that interesting, and it needs to be decided by the end of the week. Would you mind using your professional art-talking skills to help decide whether any of these applications deserve a shot?"

"I just spent all of yesterday grading three classes' worth of essays," she groaned. "Need to celebrate now."

"Please? Name a price that I can write off."

She narrowed her eyes.

"Gimme the afternoon to review them, then we hit two-for-one sake hour at Okanjo's, and you let me count this as a fellowship on my CV."

I readily agreed, and she swept our stacks of paper off the desk into her messenger bag, its numerous pins rattling as she did so.

"And that is why, my good man, when the revolution comes, I'll see to it that you're the last against the wall."

Decca was the leftist adjunct I'd been borrowing the occasional phrase from since back when she was just a leftist undergrad who felt a curious sympathy toward my scholastic doggie paddling. She'd since got, a Master's degree in comparative what-have-yous from UMass Amherst and published a book of critical essays whose jacket featured quotes of advance praise from Anis Shivani (which she assured me was rare) and advance derision from Camille Paglia (which she said wasn't especially rare but did show that the book was on the right side of history.) Suffice to say I trusted her distaste, and often appreciated the manner in which she expressed it.

Presently, she was teaching two undergrad courses each at TSU and Smith College. Presently in the more immediate sense, she was shaking the last drops from an upside-down sake bottle as I read a section from one of her class' papers. "Chinua Achebe and Reverse Racism in the Modern Essay," I said aloud in my best Boston accent. We were fortunately the only ones dining on the small second floor; otherwise we'd have been getting a healthy glower from anybody named Fitzy within earshot.

I concluded the paragraph and raised inquiring brows to Decca.

"To be fair, that one does fall towards the lower end of the curve," she said while disassembling a section of her Hampshire College roll—whitefish and two different mushrooms—to consume in tiny pieces. "But he's getting a B-minus because I don't want his parents calling the dean to complain about the radical bitch preventing their baby from fulfilling the minimum requirements for his Comm degree."

"It's really not like you to just take it easy on white dudes, present company excluded."

"A: You're a low-impact Patty Hearst experiment. B: He at least composed his own poor arguments instead of block-quoting some libertarian blog. I'll give credit where it's due, and either way, Ratemyprofessor.com doesn't have an appeals process for negative reviews. It's only a matter of time until tenure committees start taking social media into account."

I finished my drink and pushed some tiny plates to one side of the table, making room for the business portion of the evening.

"So what's your appraisal of our applications, Fellow Decca? Do I have to address you like that now?"

"No, and poor, in reverse order. Since I know the Foundation consists of pretty much just you and there isn't really a board of directors, it means there's only our two votes in the decision process. It's all goose eggs in my column, so you're in practically the same place you were this afternoon."

"I see. Should I assume that I wouldn't be particularly interested in the ones I haven't read yet?"

"Unless paying someone to construct a big pyramid made of freeze-dried grasshoppers appeals to you..."

"Was that really one of them?"

She nodded, and set the folder of applications on the table. I rested my head in my hands. I could practically feel my spirits lower themselves at the thought of being associated with something like that.

"The Withers Furniture Presents: Local Art Gallery isn't as bad as these applications imply, is it?"

"Nooo," Decca said, drawing out the vowel a bit. "You're inoffensive, midbrow, mostly free of hyphenated descriptors." I felt a little reassured by this instance of parallel thinking. "And these sorts of wacky projects aren't nearly your wheelhouse. Did you drop off flyers at an Amanda Palmer concert or something?"

Oh.

"I've no idea where this crop of applicants came from," I said.

"How far through the stack did you get?"

"I made it to the purple wall."

Decca snickered. "Yeah, if you didn't like the idea of a big fence with that gutter-but-stars Oscar Wilde quote written on it a dozen different times, you wouldn't have liked anything past it. That was comparatively a conceptual high water mark."

"Then I'll defer to your judgment."

"Not a looker in the bunch. Ship 'em off." She pushed the folder across the table to me. I could make out some red ink bleeding through on the topside, which wasn't there when she took the stack from me.

"Did you *correct* them?"

She smiled with one side of her mouth, accompanied by a slight shrug. "Force of habit. Buut— if you wanted to send their applications back to them, I think they'd really get a lot out of a more horizontal approach to grant writing like this."

After a few seconds of as blank an expression as I could muster, she continued: "Nothing on the level of our drunken cattiness goes in to the margins, it's all phrased constructively. They'll fail better next time."

"Before we even consider that—"

"I've considered it. Put it to the board—all in favor?" She raised an arm. A passing waiter assumed she was trying to flag him down, and she took the opportunity to order us another bottle of sake.

"But even aside from that, what are we going to do about the grant they aren't getting?" I said.

She pursed her lips briefly, looking off in thought.

"We could have a secondary lightning round of applications next week. Make it an in-person thing where they show up from ten to five and pitch their idea to us. Set up a webcam and call it Pioneer Valley Idol."

This seemed rather out of line with her usual stance on art and the various sakes for which it's done, though she had a remarkable ability to keep a straight face while pulling someone's leg. But still, I was worried about wrapping the review process up in time, and wondered if something attention-grabbing might be a little side bonus for the gallery. I steepled my fingers in thought.

"Oh God, you aren't actually considering that, are you?" She put another cup of sake on my side of the folder.

"What else are we going to do?"

"The same thing the NEA does: nepotize!" She clinked her cup with mine before taking a healthy sip.

"Come again?"

"You know people whose work you like, and I know people whose work you'd probably like if I showed it to you, and maybe explained what it is they're doing. Let's each come up with a list over the next day or two, then compare them and choose a winner." She finished her glass. "Sorry to bruise your conviction, but that's how all the grant writers I've known would tell you it works behind the scenes."

My spirits lowered themselves yet again, and my stomach knotted from more than just the lukewarm sushi.

I spent the following morning huddled in an overstuffed chair at the cafe where all the baristas looked like someone's Quirky Best Friend from a 1980's romantic comedy, picking at an oversized scone and weighing my options.

I had read over Decca's marginalia as a precaution and she wasn't wrong in her criticisms, at least as far as I understood them. So, I was left trying to decide who among my circle of acquaintances would be getting short-listed for the year's grant.

Myra was right out. I wasn't entirely sure if we had a rule against past recipients being eligible, but that just seemed wrong. More wrong than I had already and was planning to be again with this endeavor.

Verrick was a possibility, though I didn't really know much about the man himself. I'd only met him once, very briefly, the first time he'd inquired about showing his work in the gallery. He wasn't rude per se, but he had a definite air of wanting to stop being around people, and subsequent transactions had all been handled through couriers. Potentially not the sort of guy who'd appreciate any amount of press coverage. Nevertheless, I had his contact info and he was first on the list.

Further candidates were more difficult to line up. I didn't display anything in the gallery that I didn't like, but I didn't really know if any of it was interesting enough to try and boost up to Next Big Thing status. There were plenty of slightly unusual portraits and photos of buildings in shadow out there already, and if I was going to be shoving money an artist's way, I figured it might as well be the sort of artist who stood a chance of having a movement named after them.

I imagined an entry in a textbook, next to a picture of the gallery: *It was due to the influence of the Withers Furniture Presents: Local Art Gallery that -----ism developed in the early years of the 21st century...*

After being lost in that thought for some indeterminate period of time, I overheard a familiar voice repeating an intricately-adjectived order to the barista. I groffled the last corner of my scone and turned to see Ian Irvin at the counter stirring his, ah, coffee for short. I waved a red and white videogame proposal to get his attention.

"Greg Withers, of all the dudes to find today," he shouted across the shop, then came over to sit backwards on a wooden chair across from me.

Ian, Another TSU alum, majored in film. His first feature out of college, *The Fire That Refines Him*, was picked up by an independent film festival and won a few prestigious-sounding awards, so he'd been out of town for some months showing it off at other festivals and doing the whole rubbing-elbows sort of thing that one does with festival people. He reached into his jacket pocket and fanned out a handful of industry insiders' business cards for proof, as though I were supposed to close my eyes and pick one and he'd magically predict it was the Duplass Brothers.

I'd thought his film was the maundering sort of indie flick that has too many scenes of twenty-somethings sitting on roofs looking wistfully at sunsets, but I liked him enough as a person and I was glad to see a buddy doing well.

I told him about my recent endeavors with the W.A.I.F. and the grant quagmire, during which he helped himself to a sheet from the rejection folder and examined it. "How do you manage to write so neat so small?"

"That's all Decca's hand."

"Who?"

"Decca Lyne, from TSU. You might have had a class with her, or a negative review if you read the semesterly arts journal."

"That chick who always talked like a Bad Religion album, right? What's you guys' deal with these?"

"Those are the applications we're passing on."

"You don't want to fund this pop-up restaurant with only two tables where they each place the other table's order? Seriously?"

"We're trying to fund art, and that doesn't really say anything. I mean, other than liability once someone with a food allergy sits down."

"Art doesn't have to say anything, it just has to get attention. Maybe a little anaphylaxis will get people looking you guys' way."

"They'd be looking at some lady turning purple and wheezing like an excited pug because somebody sent her shellfish, followed by looking at my picture beneath the headline 'Idle Rich Funds Murder comma Spectacle.'"

"Just say it's a commentary; total get-out-of-expectations-free card. I saved Fire's hide with that one during a panel at NOIFF. Saying that about anything you've done turns it into the sort of art people would install Plexiglass over if it was painted on the side of a building overnight."

"What was the movie commenting on?"

"Nobody ever asks, that's the magic of it! Just like how nobody asks what that Eliot quote I used for the title means."

I nodded and made a contemplative chin-furrow, though I didn't think his methodology was all that honest. Honesty, I thought, was one of the big things that auteurs were lauded for having in their films; at least the ones that didn't involve loopy time-travel. But I wasn't in a confrontational mood. Fortunately, I'd discovered a certain phrase to deploy in situations at the gallery where I needed to respond to something but couldn't come up with anything substantial to say. I figured it wasn't really a blow-off, since everybody I used it on actually wound up reading something in to it.

"There's some human truth in there."

"Truth there is: know how to play your audience." He slipped the application back into the folder and leaned forward. "So what does it take to make it to round two?"

"Pardon?"

"Let me put in a bid for this grant of yours. I need to do

something after *Fire*'s fest success, and the whole indie thing is still in vogue. What would be indier than making a whole film using one little arts grant?"

I wasn't sure that was how one properly measured indieness, but I was admittedly strapped for ideas at that point.

"Can you actually do that?"

"If we make it a found-footage setup, yeah. Those are dirt cheap, but getting kind of played out at this point. Could do a documentary about art around here, work a little keepin'-it-local into the mix while showing my sensitive side. A little something that will get me called 'bold and dynamic' in the press. Just give me the word and I'll figure out what we can do when we get the budget in place. What do you say?"

I quickly considered the potential prestige of being associated with an up-and-coming auteur's new project. Even if I didn't care much for his work, which did violate my personal principle with the gallery a bit, it could potentially bring us to more of the world's attention; letting us give future grant recipients an even bigger hand.

It was due to the influence of the Withers Furniture Presents: Local Art Gallery that the thrifty tour-de-force techniques of 'maundercore' filmmaking developed in the early years of the 21st century...

I swallowed a slight feeling that I was making one of those soul-selling sorts of deals you had to sign with your own blood and told him I'd put it to the board.

2

It should be said that my parents, who'd established the Withers Furniture Presents: Local Art Gallery *and* let me start the Withers Art & Inspiration Foundation, were very hands-off philanthropists.

On his way to becoming the second largest mattress retailer in Western Massachusetts, my father often voiced a desire to "do the Carnegie thing" and help facilitate cultural goings-on with spare wealth when he made it big. Since one can only make so much bigness from furniture sales in the Bostonless half of the state, my mother suggested they begin their philanthropic ventures with enough of a trust to fund a small art gallery instead of a couple thousand libraries. The gallery opened three years ago, coincidentally just a few months after I'd graduated from TSU with a degree in nothing in particular.

I assume Carnegie wasn't averse to nepotism either,

what with all the kids he must have had.

They didn't particularly care what I did with the gallery as long as it was well regarded and getting used. While I wasn't particularly well-versed in the arts beyond what I absorbed in required college courses, the gallery seemed to be relatively self-sustaining with frequent print sales to incoming students at the Six Colleges looking to make their dorm walls a little less taupe, as well as the occasional commission from the sale of an original piece.

I, however, wasn't content to just live off of my parents' largess. I came up with the idea for the W.A.I.F. to sort of make my own mark on the world, with the side benefit of giving Treebridge's surplus humanities majors something to put their degrees towards without moving to New York. When I'd mentioned that to a sous chef friend of mine, he said it would probably do wonders for waitstaff turnover rates, so I thought it would definitely be worth undertaking a venture with such broad economic impact.

As the grant was my pet project, I decided I needed to take a firm hand with Decca on the matter of Ian. Not to get all do-as-I-say about it, but to maintain some degree of personal control over the thing. Even if the direction it was taking felt a little underhanded, at least it was my own hand being undered. I just hoped Decca would take the news somewhat in stride.

I'd witnessed several instances of her retaliating for slights against her in the past—most vividly, her overturning of the refreshments table at a TSU Democratic Alliance meeting after they had decided not to oppose Army recruiters visiting the campus. Her minor black-blocking hamstrung the group for that semester as most of the meeting then left in search of another club whose Stop & Shop deli trays were better secured, regardless of club ideology. I thought she currently regarded me more highly than she did college Democrats, but I was still a bit worried about the uprightness of my desk in case the discussion took a bad turn.

I firmly braced myself for the encounter by the time she arrived, and we went in to my office. She pulled a notebook from her pin-clad messenger bag.

"So," she began, "there's a painter in Agawam who's working with—"

I held up an opened hand, hoping it was one of the less dickish ways to let someone know you needed to talk over them.

"Fortunate circumstances have led to a slight change of plans, and I think I've already determined who the recipient will be. Ian Irvin."

"The hell?" She flopped her notebook down onto the desk. "You really think he's the shape of art to come?"

"I ran in to him earlier. He'd mentioned he was looking to make another film, and I thought if we were to provide the funding then it might get the gallery a bit more—"

"It'll get us shoved in to the same gormless niche as his cloying little slack-flick."

I was taken aback by the language, but glad it wasn't directed at me.

"There's a niche for that?"

"Oooh yeah. Big niche of aimless twenty-somethings with oodles of self-regard and about as much expressive talent as a dry heave. You've probably noticed a lot more crayons getting used in the design of movie posters as of late."

I supposed there were, now that she'd brought it up, but had just assumed it was a clever cost-cutting tactic.

"That symptom's usually coterminous with more whispery-singing acoustic guitarists playing inside venues rather than out on the street corners where they belong, which we're also lousy with at the moment," she said. "Soon enough, those venues won't offer a single cocktail without basil in it."

"This is getting a little outside of the point," I said. "Ian wants to do something different from *The Fire that Refines Him* for his next film. Maybe he was just doing the indie thing to establish himself before branching out."

Decca rested her chin in an open hand.

"Did he say he was doing that, or are you just assuming the best intentions on his part because you used to play Halo together?"

"Words to that effect were spoken by him, yes."

"You're sure he wasn't winking or anything? Both his hands visible at the time, fingers uncrossed?"

"Just because he's an auteur doesn't mean he's one of those insane kinds who'll drown his actors or lie to friends."

"He doesn't have to be insane, just a prig. Which he, well, you've seen his movie. It's like someone copied a bunch of Chuck Klosterman articles onto a sheet of Silly Putty then fed it in to a projector."

I considered asking her to explain that, but I could figure out its intent from her tone.

"I didn't like it too much either, really, but just because we're catching his elevator doesn't mean we need to get off at the same floor. We can just get a little boost, and use the exposure to find a bigger audience for our other artists."

"Like a leech that decides to vomit half of its meals out at the local Red Cross."

I balked, or at least took on the expression of what I thought balking looked like. Taken aback, at the very least.

"Am I really being a parasite with this plan?"

Decca sighed, then folded her arms in front of her.

"No. Well, yes, but not maliciously. I think it would be better to stand on our own and actually get stuff done with what we have, rather than hope to catch residual spotlight from some bandwagoner; but you have a valid reason for wanting the gallery to find a larger audience. It's your call, but Ian is honestly a boor."

I could tell by her tone that she still wasn't pleased, and felt I'd somehow betrayed her. I probably should have expected such a reaction from someone who was still part of a scene where accusations of selling out were serious business. In addition to her friendship, I very much needed someone around who had a more thorough knowledge about this grant business than I did. I didn't even realize we should have had a board of directors until she pointed it out.

"Do you still want to be my fellow?"

"I don't want to be involved with the actual grant process, if that's what you're going through with. That's all on you. But, you do still need a bunch of back-end stuff if you want to be a serious foundation, and the experience will read the same on my CV whether it's something I feel invested in or not." There was a sing-song kind of tone to the second half of that sentence which felt particularly knife-twisting. "I'll just cloister off from the decision-making process and work on writing us a chimerical bombination of a mission statement while you're herding Michael Bay State around." She flashed a dubious smile, then stood and turned on her heels with a little wave. "Bon soir!"

I stood up from my chair, but didn't follow her for fear of getting berated with large words in a public area. "The presentation ceremony's on Tuesday. Please do come," I said after her, which was met with a thumbs-up over her shoulder without breaking stride. Pretty sure it was a thumb.

Either way, the matter was settled, and I flipped through my Rolodex (antiquated, I know, but so many artists have pretty business cards) to find Ian's number and give him the news, sans Decca-logue.

Prior to opening the gallery the following morning, I stopped by Myra's to let her know the plans she was hopefully to be included in; and see if she might have some new work of hers to unveil at the ceremony as well. I'd already scheduled someone calling themselves a "neo-vorticist" to replace the swoopy inks who had one fewer painting than they did, and I didn't want any more confusion over empty spaces during an event.

Ian informed me that his current plan was to make a documentary about the local art scene, focusing on Myra and her creative process, which felt like it was steering the gallery towards the self-absorption I was hoping to avoid. I didn't want to piss Decca off in vain, and I wasn't at all curious about what sort of wrath Ian could muster if I decided to drop him. The only question was what particular form his project would take, and that was blessedly out of my hands.

Myra's apartment building was a converted factory along the Connecticut river, the sort with enormous echoing hallways and deep furrows still set into the floors; protected by thick varnish and a collective appreciation for the impression of authenticity. It also still had the old industrial elevators with only wire mesh separating riders from the shaft walls, in working order, which I'd always thought were fun to ride in. The elevator itself wasn't quite as large as some of her statues I'd seen, which left me wondering if she had some sort of pulley system outside her window. Likely hand-made if it existed, as the making of things was kind of her forte. During our senior year, she'd both built and taught me how to pronounce a trebuchet. Completely on a whim; not even for a class project or out of anger over a Sox game, although it was eventually enlisted for the latter purpose.

We'd first met one day during sophomore year when I was attempting to walk across campus and happened upon an impromptu performance-art-slash-immersive-theatre event taking place on the sidewalk. There were a handful of people standing in a loose crowd wearing old-timey costumes, with a few of their number wearing papier-mâché animal heads. Most of them were gesticulating or possibly acting out scenes while reciting I had no idea what. One dapper, crow-headed fellow was trying to drag a woman by one leg while she attempted to claw towards the sidewalk. One man simply stood on a large cardboard leaf with an evergreen wreath suspended around his thighs by fishing line. I didn't at all get what was going on, but I'd spent enough time in the Six College area to recognize when art was afoot. I sat down on a bench at the edge of the scene that was shared by a bored-looking woman in Victorian dress, and unwittingly blurred the line between art and observer.

"How long's this thing been going on for?" I said to her.

"Technically since 1934, I think."

"Oh." I observed the goings-on for a moment. A man with what I think was an armadillo on his back was handing pamphlets to people on the sidewalk, most of whom deposited them in to a trashcan he was conveniently located near. "What's taking so long?"

"Hypersigils don't just invoke themselves, whatever those are. Though the whole thing's off the rails at this point anyways. I was supposed to be dancing with this guy with a doorknocker on his forehead, but he ran off to buy the group more Djarum Blacks just before we started. So, the rest of the group is just carrying on doing whatever the fuck and it isn't going to work without me and him in place. Even Dada had its rules, but try telling that to anybody in America who pronounces 'artist' with an E at the end when describing themselves. This isn't art, it's suicide in a social way."

I wasn't quite sure what most of that was supposed to mean, but I responded with, "There's some human truth in that."

"Yeah, I'll certainly give it that."

"Is there a storyline or anything I should know about while watching?"

She leaned to the side and made that theatrical getting-the-vapours pose, laying the back of her wrist across her forehead. "We open on the world's only visual artist who doesn't smoke, disillusioned with interdisciplinary movements and eager to make things on a professional basis, torn between her dread at the impending destruction of her finely-crafted bird masks by campus security and the recent discovery that she'd kind of like to see the artless twits wearing them get wailed on."

"That does sound pretty dramatic," I said, having taken her entirely at face value.

She raised an eyebrow and started to say something, but stopped and pointed to the scene with a single sharp laugh.

A TSU-branded golf cart had pulled up and a middle-aged security officer stepped out. He approached the edge of the scene and announced, "Move along ya fuckin' homos," while hovering a hand over his billy club holster like a cowboy preparing for a showdown. The wreath-wearing performer was the first to break, and he promptly tripped over his own costume while attempting to run and was overtaken by the officer.

"Exit, pursued by a Statie," she said.

"Did you really make those costumes?"

"The nice parts. Lemme tell you about them on the way to wherever you were headed. I could do with some more guileless acquaintances after those schmucks."

Our friendship was formalized in the dining hall, which offered a nice view of eight or nine undergrad theatre majors failing to overpower a single part-time security guard.

I exited the elevator once it clunked up to her floor, walked down the big echo-y hallway and knocked on Myra's apartment door. Shortly afterwards, I was greeted with a friendly hug draped in a smock that had unfortunately seen recent use against a bunch of blue paint. Myra apologized and invited me in. Her apartment was a rather large open area that served as both living room and studio space, with a kitchen separated by a breakfast bar off to one side and doors leading to a bedroom and bathroom on the opposite wall.

"So, what have you been up to aside from whatever you were working on a second ago?" I said.

"Nothing much of note. Had an Internet date last night that fizzled out shortly after the typical no-what-do-you-*really*-do line of questioning, and I needed to vent by doing what I really do. So, uh, sorry that your shirt got caught up in the drama." She tossed a roll of paper towels over to me from the kitchen side of the room. "So what brings you by?" she asked.

"A couple of things—the first of which was wondering if you happen to have anything new I could display in the gallery for next Tuesday, which I think you might have already answered." I glanced around a little, unable to tell what might have been a work in progress and what might have just been a chair or shelf, which involved in numerous accidents like my own.

"Sure do! The morning's frustrations are on that stand by the window." She hopped up to sit on the counter, leaving blue handprints on it as she did, then slid her legs around into the living room and pointed towards an object, which was mostly the same color as the blotch on my shirt. She then asked a delicate question for one in my line of work: "What do you think?"

I thought, after a moment's observation, that her sculpture looked like a rampant cat made entirely out of corners, which did look pretty cool, but I couldn't tell her that. Not just because it wasn't what she wanted to hear, but because I was accustomed to keeping up the appearance of someone who didn't think a corner-y cat was just about its angular/feline nature. While most of the artistic process was completely alien to me, I knew most sculptors weren't inclined to sculpt things that were *about* whatever they happened to look like. I could recognize on some base level that there were more things going on with Myra's sculpture, but whatever they may have been were indecipherable to my eye. And so the facade was maintained by reflex.

"There's a certain human truth about it."

"You seem say that about stuff you don't get," she said. Now that I think of it, she might actually have been the one I'd originally adopted that phrase from way back when.

"And I mean it every time," I said. "I don't think it's a bad thing. The human truth, I mean—not my not getting it."

"Well, what human truth do you allegedly see in this statue?" She dropped from the counter and stood with her hands on her hips, no discernible expression beneath the gesso drying across part of her face.

"That's not fair." I said. "Nobody else ever follows up like that. You're just supposed to nod appreciatively and then one of the other guests chimes in with something about its vulnerability or resonance, then by the time she's done talking there's an hors d'oeuvre in my mouth so it'd be rude to speak."

"Do you at least like it?"

"Of course I do," I said. "It looks really neat how it sort of juts out all over like that." I do try to be constructive for artsy friends.

"Such insight."

"I'm sure people who do think about statues will find thinkable things in it. The only hand I have in the matter is deciding whether they get to think about it on my property; which they certainly will."

She smiled, and inadvertently wiped paint across the other side of her face trying to cover it.

"Cool enough to find a spot in the exhibition, eh?"

"I've got just the place for it, right between a photo of bicycles with snow on them, and a fire alarm, which may actually just be an old piece of installation art now that I think of it."

"Thanks, Greg. You're a pal, even if you aren't up to code."

"Will... ahem," I gestured towards the statue.

"*Memories Dull my Senses*," she said, making air quotes as she did so.

"Will Memories be complete by then?"

"It's pretty much done as it is." She walked up to the statue, examined it a moment, then took a nearby paintbrush and flicked its bristles to speckle pale dots across the probably-a-cat. "Hm. New development. Give me a day or two, but yeah, definitely by Tuesday."

"Great! Second point of business, ah, you should know that the exhibition will feature an announcement of the next year's grant recipient who you may or may not want your work associated with."

She stopped regarding the statue to cock an eyebrow at me.

"Are you giving it to Staind in honor of their significant contributions to Western Massachusetts culture?"

"No! What do you take me for?"

"Can't be that bad, then. With whom am I sharing the honor of your patronage?"

"Have you seen *The Fire that Refines Him*?"

"Yeah, just like everybody else who graduated with the director, but I couldn't tell you the difference between it and *Garden State*. I actually might have just seen one of them two separate times. Which one had that scene of the guy alone on a playground at night watching a meteor shower from the top of a slide, and then he just leans back and falls in tandem with a giant shooting star when the music hits a crescendo?"

"That scene was just in *Fire*, I believe."

"Figures. I recognized that playground from some local urban decay photosets."

"Either way, how would you like to take part in a documentary about your artistic process and vision?" I said.

"It would be by the guy who did that movie, you mean."

"Yep." I nodded for emphasis.

She opened her mouth slightly, hesitated, then loosed another volley of paint at her statue and tilted her head to examine it.

"He seems like a bore, honestly," she eventually said.

I'd expected as much from Decca, but this was honestly out of left field. I suppose I just lacked the proper artist mindset, as I'd never been sure of how to anticipate Myra's aesthetic preferences.

"I mean, he's certainly not—whichever school of sculpture you're working in here, but Ian says he's looking to get a little dynamic with his next project. Your stuff is dynamic! This thing kinda looks like it's lunging."

She placed her brush into a smock pocket and crossed her arms before her, still facing the statue.

"It kinda does, doesn't it? Though I think of it more as looming than lunging; something just sinister and waiting there instead of suddenly coming up at you."

I found myself thinking of it that way, too, when she brought it up, but didn't get what the speckles contributed to that. But there were more pressing matters at hand.

"So do you want to let Ian feature you in the documentary, history of boredom notwithstanding?"

"I wouldn't have to really do anything for it, right? Just answer some questions and let him point the camera at my stuff for what ever the runtime needs to be? I can at least guarantee any boredom that results won't be due to my involvement."

"Well, I suppose 'why not' is a form of 'yes.'"

"That might as well have been under Ian's photo in our yearbook."

I was used to abridging other people's messages before passing them on to Ian at that point.

With her approval secured, I excused myself and left her to her work; hoofing it downtown past the shriveled, dishwater-gray snow banks still clinging to curbsides despite the flagrant sunshine. I supposed it was vaguely metaphoric, as I wasn't feeling all that enthused by the course things were taking.

Even if my plan wasn't the best of all possible plans, I reassured myself, it was at least going along smoothly now. I felt on the verge of whistling an upbeat tune to try and prod myself in to better spirits, or at least tipping a street musician to play one as I made my way through town; but after a couple different ditties I requested from musicians with clarinets, overturned plastic buckets, and some sort of bulbous harp-guitar along my route, I was still pensive about my choices and suddenly lacking in pocket change.

I stopped in a coffee shop along the way that I knew took cards and, as an odd bit of good fortune, saw they had on their wall a small oil-on-something by Donald Verrick, which I hadn't seen before titled "*This Parade Leading Nowhere.*"

I'd appreciated it while waiting in line for a few moments before noticing that next to it on the shop's community corkboard was a smallish Manifestian thesis titled "Notes Toward the Disinterment Heretofore of Place and Subject: A Riposte" which made frequent references to "such conceptual folderol as you see to your right." I asked the Quirky Best Friend behind the counter, and she said it was posted just a matter of days after the shop displayed the painting.

Apparently as an addendum to the typed manifesto, someone wrote, "But both of those things are there you tiny manikins," in small crabbed handwriting below the title. I didn't quite grasp the point of the paper, and never was one to stifle the free exchange of ideas, but I left with my coffee hoping the thing would soon be covered over by a flyer for guitar lessons.

I spent that evening at O'Hennessey's during their acoustic open mic night, engaging in a spirited round of not talking to people and generally contemplating my role in things.

My possible status as a lowly Sundance Remora was the dominant thought of the night, as Decca's accusations still weighed heavy on my mind. I felt in a mood fit to be shot with high-contrast lighting and deep shadows with a Tom Waits soundtrack in some film, presumably one that was better directed than *The Fire that Refines Him*.

I didn't think he was all that interesting of a filmmaker, but other people seemed to. Then again, Decca often made more sense than other people, but should putting art out there for an audience take into account that audience's pre-existing taste? Decca and Myra would both have different variations on "no" for that question, I felt certain. I was already violating standard procedure by not taking my own preferences into account, but it was in service of being able to give my future preferences more of an account than I could at present.

My folks seemed to be happy with the gallery's current level of operations, though it still felt like I should be doing more for the artists we displayed—beyond providing foot traffic with complimentary cheese every season or so. It seemed I should do what I could to help the artists starve less.

I'd once tried asking the owner of what I'd thought was another local gallery who featured blown-glass vases and pendants about what is expected of a proper art gallery operator, but it turned out the place was actually just a jewelry store with a really sparse interior. The local museums weren't much help, since the majority of their collection was simply on loan from the estates of artists who had long since stopped caring about renown and profit. More so than living ones, I mean.

It did have, if not an actual working artist's enthusiastic approval, a lack of her outright disapproval, and she was one of few others whose taste I'd come to trust when unable to form my own.

To give myself a break from introspecting, I took in the details of the bar, evaluating the other complaints leveled against Ian's encroaching scene. There was, as predicted, a very much white guitarist with an affected rasp in his voice playing an acoustic Outkast cover on stage whom I was not inclined to listen to. On the plus side, the gimlet I'd ordered was entirely basil-free.

Maybe Decca's fears were exaggerated. How much damage could an indie film do? Ian certainly didn't seem like he'd be the volatile Troy Duffy style of director.

The guitarist transitioned in to a faux-soulful Salt-N-Pepa cover after an attempt at audience banter fell flat, and I hurried home so as not to miss the new episode of "Mario Lopez at Large." He was to be in Sumatra that week.

3

The weekend passed with no significant hiccups in the process of grant giving and gallery-arranging. Decca, while still not at all enthused by the prospect of Ian's film, had seen her way to producing a deceptively professional mission statement for the gallery's website. Then, upon actually looking at our website, set out to find us a competent web designer to renovate it. I offered to find some flashing "UNDER CONSTRUCTION" images for it in the meantime, which was met with a roll of her eyes and not brought up again. Things were curt and kept to professional matters, but we hadn't totally fallen out.

Myra's statue was put in place after she'd painted over the speckles I saw her apply.

I'd only spoken with Ian over the phone during that period, but he'd assured me that he and his people (I had thought the fame threshold for someone having "people" would be much higher) were busy getting things in order to start the actual filmmaking process soon after the announcement; whatever that actually involved. I envisioned a lot of sunglassed people on cellphones saying *ciao*.

The morning of the event was spent quibbling with caterers, ensuring the hors d'oeuvres were appropriately restrained—nothing too sauce-covered or carefully balanced on a delicate papery cracker. I could easily imagine someone gesturing with a Swedish meatball too close to a painting, and I prided myself on not displaying the kind of paintings where a gravy stain would just blend right in. That's one thing I knew the Manifestians were wrong about in regards to me, whatever the rest of their criticisms might mean. No Rothko. *Never* Rothko.

It was around five o'clock that Decca showed up in the closest thing to evening wear I could recall seeing her in, though her presence would have been bolstering even if she'd been wearing half of a band tee roughly sewn to half of a different band tee. We sat on a bench near the neo-vorticism, which was also near a table where the caterers were setting up a beverage station, and proceeded to shoot the breeze.

"Ready for the big reveal?" she asked, making a show of sneaking a plastic cup of white wine off the table which would have been free anyways.

"Ready as can be, I suppose. Invitations were sent out, a quarter-page ran in the alt weekly. I had an email from a UMass professor asking if they could give class credit for attending; I didn't see why not."

"I'm surprised—we don't usually bother to ask." She fidgeted with her lone earring, which was actually a very small padlock. "I put up some flyers around my campuses for what good that'd do. Highlighted 'refreshments' on them."

"Anything to swell out the ranks and dilute the usual crowd. I think the announcing of Ian might appeal to a less stodgy demographic than the fine arts usually attract."

"Eh, they're about as stodgy, they just stodge about different things."

The conversation was still a little strained after our argument, so I sought an opportunity to relieve tension with a point of mutual interest. More than colleagues, more than friends, we were both full-blooded New Englanders, and I knew we needed a third party for bonding on that level to take place.

Our first group of guests—three men and two women, older, dressed nicer than street clothes—had arrived. One was glancing around with his jacket in hand, cluing me in to them being "society" types. I rose and made my way over to do the gracious host thing with my fellow in tow.

"I don't know if you could get stodgier than some of these folks. Observe," I whispered to her in a conspiratorial tone.

"Oh?"

I approached the group with my hand extended and that first man met it with his jacket.

"We, um, don't have a coat check, sir, sorry. I'm the proprietor, Greg Withers. Welcome to our spring opening!"

He draped his jacket over one arm with an air of resignation and gave my hand a brief shake. More like a hop. The women and one of the men greeted us with congenial inclinations of their heads and mouthed hellos, while the other man didn't acknowledge us and seemed a little scared of the place.

"Pleasure to make your acquaintance," said the jacket-holder, who didn't so much smile or frown as simply present his teeth.

Decca then extended her hand, and received the same hand-hop-and-tooth-showing before we apparently ceased to exist and the group turned to saunter amongst the exhibits.

We returned to the bench and when the group was far enough away Decca whispered, "Did they *have* names?"

"I don't know them personally, but I recognized their type. They might not have set foot in here before, but once invitations to an event start appearing in the right social circles they'll show up just to be seen. They do actually buy art on occasion, usually for their offices or to impress other people who don't actively like art, so they just have to be put up with. Though I don't know what that tooth display was about."

"Maybe he's just too above plebeian displays of bonhomie to bother contorting the edges of his mouth," Decca said while affecting a posh Frasier accent, "or maybe he was soliciting a place in the gallery for 'em."

"I don't think they really had the... level of craft we've come to expect from our artists."

Decca suppressed a laugh through a mouthful of Yellowtail. "Not really gallery-quality teeth, no. Maybe fit to go up on the wall at Applebee's."

Many people might say that the most popular pastime in New England is baseball, and that may be the impression we give to outsiders. But in truth, a far more popular hobby amongst born-and-bred New Englanders, at least the sort who can actually trace their lineage back to Old Englanders, is what we've come to refer to as "recreational classism."

A significant cornerstone of Decca's and my friendship was formed when we discovered we were both varsity players while sitting in the back row of some writing course at TSU, directly behind a middle-aged returning student who kept going on weird personal tangents during class time, and a 17-year old who seemed to be under the impression that she was the first person in the history of Western civilization to have taken a summer vacation to Barcelona. There's nothing outright malicious behind it, just sort of a private-ish flexing of observational muscle. My theory is that it's a reflex left over from the days when we were a bunch of small Pilgrim colonies all condemning one another at the drop of a belted hat.

Regardless of its origins, I was glad she and I were still on good enough terms to be Northern together.

After a mischievous glance out the bay window, Decca leaned over and whispered, "Don't look now, but somebody just got off of a shift selling newspapers in 1920." She nudged an elbow towards the door, where a bearded fellow our age wearing a garish plaid driving cap and suspenders over a t-shirt had just entered. He was with some people who I could tell at a glance were probably artist-types, since their number included a girl who was wearing a skirt made out of old men's' ties, though they weren't ones I could remember having met before. I went over to greet them when I finished laughing in to a handkerchief at Decca's remark.

I extended a hand and introduced myself as I reached their little group. My gregariousness was met with, "Is Ian here yet?" followed by them making a beeline to the refreshments table when I told them he had yet to arrive. Decca, with social hackles raised, sauntered over to a small encaustics display when she noticed them approaching.

I thought it a little odd at first, since I hadn't mentioned Ian as the grant recipient in any promotional material, but I guess it was fine if Ian had mentioned it to friends of his. Or his people.

Ian's fans were followed soon by several other small groups of attendees whom I did my best to greet with repetitive congeniality. Several were artists I was acquainted with. Two or three I recognized from local media, though they seemed to be there on personal time rather than professionally—without camera bags or the like. Eventually Myra arrived and greeted me with a thankfully paint-free hug.

"Looks like you've got a healthy mix of students and upper-middle townies," she said.

"More of a crowd than I was expecting by this point. Though I certainly can't complain about younger demographics taking an interest in the arts. If that's what they're actually here for."

"Yeah, about that, what's Ian want with all those insurance waivers?"

I stood processing that for a second, which cued her in to the fact that I hadn't the slightest idea what she was on about. She continued:

"He called and came by my place earlier asking me to sign a handful of small print forms with severe titles like 'Release of Liability.' Has he blindsided you with anything like that?"

"No, I think I'm the one with forms for him to sign before we make this project public. Maybe it was just a standard pre-documentary don't-sue-us-if-you-look-bad thing."

She shrugged.

Decca then appeared by my side saying, at somewhat more than a whisper, "There's some self-described 'bloggerix' over there who only speaks in sentences she's heard on TV. Parajournalism finally has its own Peter Travers!" She held one empty plastic wine cup with a second one nested inside of it.

"Pardon?" Myra said.

"This is the foundation's new fellow, Decca Lyne. This is my friend Myra Pavonine."

They shared a perfunctory handshake.

"You're the one making those jerky statues, right?" Decca asked.

"Excuse me?" Myra angled her head to one side, taking on one of those odd smiles that doesn't actually look amused.

"Jerky like, crooked and jaggy. Not jerky like those guys over there," Decca thumbed over her shoulder towards the newsie who'd asked for Ian. "It's an interesting aesthetic. Disruptive in a way that calls more attention to what it disrupts than to itself, a more confident approach than that giant fuckoff mommy spider the ICA is displaying on the other side of the state."

Myra's smile shifted to a more genuine one. "Why thank you," she said. "I've personally always thought Louise Bourgeois' later works to be a little—"

I nodded appreciatively at the conclusion of that sentence, though I completely blanked on the terms d'art she brought to bear. Her tone seemed disapproving, however.

"Well, she has bougie right there in her name," Decca said when Myra finished. "Guess it's only natural that she'd concern herself with—" More graduate-level vocabulary followed.

They were clearly over my head at that point, so I detached from their conversation and began circulating among patrons old and new. Ian's crowd had grown, and our reserves of merlot proportionally shrunk since I'd last observed them. Nobody spilled any hors d'oeuvres on the floor or the art, as far as I could tell. Things were proceeding as hoped.

I alighted next to a group of minor collectors I recognized who were gathered around that giant brass spire of Myra's. One older gentleman with a generous beard was holding court on its apparently numerous phallo-so-forth aspects.

"But perhaps we should ask the proprietor his thoughts on this piece, hm," said a woman in the group who'd noticed my approach. The bearded fellow gave a small nod and made a deferential hand gesture as though he'd just held open a door for me.

I was caught flat-footed, and immediately realized I wasn't holding anything with which to occupy my mouth.

"Well, I was immediately drawn to the..." My lizard brain dredged up a small bundle of jargon. "...the frank earnestness it displays." I just liked how it looked like a giant, angry coral.

My response was greeted with small, professional laughter.

"I see there's much of both Frank and Earnest in the

36

piece, as it were," said the bearded fellow, "and they're best expressed through its material composition: brazen, though with no inherent magnetism." This was followed by more small laughter.

"Indeed," I said, hopeful from the tone of things that it wasn't I who had just been zinged at a rather high altitude. "I believe the artist herself is over there if you'd like to ask her what—" Their laughter suddenly increased in magnitude and, getting a little uncomfortable, I excused myself on what seemed like a high note and headed towards the catering table. I needed to stock up on canapés before someone else had a chance to ask what I thought about other exhibits.

Unfortunately, I was intercepted en route to the hors d'oeuvres by someone who could be described as these people's exact opposite. Standing before me in uneven glasses and yesterday's stubble was Chad Marston.

"Oh, hiya Greg," he said. His posture indicated that he'd waited there for me to turn around. "Fancy meeting you here. Nice stuff you're showing off this season!"

"Thank you," I said. I couldn't recall sending him an invitation. I wondered who I knew that might have been in a position to tell him about it. Doing so would have required being in conversation with him, and most people I'd talked to seemed to know that was something to be avoided.

"Y'know, looking around, I was thinking you might want to balance out some of the louder pieces here with something a little more subdued in their presentation."

Chad Marston was a *coterie recipier*, with an accent mark over one of the letters in that second word though I swear it was a different letter each time I'd seen it. It meant that he created recipes for dishes that were meant to be read and appreciated in the manner of poems, rather than actually put to use in a kitchen. He self-published a book of his work, and for about a month solicited me about displaying poster-sized prints of his recipes in the gallery. And for appearance's sake I couldn't just tell him outright that he was a twit.

"I'd consider it, but we already have some black and white photos up. I think adding white posters with plain black text on top of that might make people feel like they walked in to an underground 'zine."

"You'll have them thinking they walked in to Granta if you'd be willing to display just a couple of my pieces to build some buzz," he began pulling a folded sheet of paper from inside his jacket pocket. "Here, look, this one's called Mista Chad's Down-Home Gumbo. I think you're gonna dig it."

Lacking an easy out, I took the paper from him and read. To his credit, he at least formatted everything like an actual cookbook instead of putting it in Cummings-y blank verse. He even included a little story about the recipe in a sidebar like in real cookbooks by fake chefs:

See here now, my grammy been workin' kitchen voodoo with this here gumbo recipe erry Sunday for us chilluns since we been knee-high to a mud bug. The secret she be usin' ain't no Tony's, ya herd...

I stopped reading there. I didn't need a thorough knowledge of either cooking or poetry to determine what was wrong with that particular food-verse.

"Chad, you're at least as white as I am."

The comment seemed to slide off of him.

"I think I really captured an authentic Southern voice in the intro, not to mention how I invoke the flavors of tradi—"

Feeling like prey, I emptied my ink sac.

"There's some human truth in there."

"Yeah, exactly!" He clasped his hands together in front of him, beaming like a third-grader who'd just got a ribbon in front of the whole auditorium.

"Let me reflect on this when things are a little less busy

and I'll—" *epiphany* "—I'll have my people get in touch with you."

"Cool, man, here's my card." He fumbled around in another pocket, which gave me the momentary distraction I needed to slip around him and dart over to the refreshments, where I folded his paper in quarters and slipped it beneath a stack of napkins.

After arming myself with a small paper plate festooned with tiny crackers and pieces of what I think was some pickled vegetable, I re-entered the fray. Decca and Myra's conversation was joined by some guy who was talking boisterously with his hands, though the two of them didn't appear to share his enthusiasm. The tooth-presenter and his crowd seemed to really like the new jagged cat, or were maybe just displaying aggression. The phallo-guy had moved his critiquing carnival over to the snow-covered bicycle photo. Art was being actively appreciated, and I hadn't noticed anybody just ducking in for some snacks then slinking out. All in all, I was pleased with the turnout.

Shortly after I recirculated, Ian entered with a couple of his people. The group who'd shown up earlier for him began whooping and applauding upon noticing his arrival; which immediately silenced the rest of the patrons who were using their inside voices. I made my way over to greet him, as he waved to the crowd.

"Greg! What's the haps," he asked, extending a hand. Beneath his corduroy blazer he was wearing a t-shirt that had, as far as I could tell, the entirety of *Dover Beach* printed on it.

I shook his hand and pulled him urgently towards my office, where I had the grant contract sitting on my desk with hopefully all instances of "Myra" and "sculpture" from the last year's version find-and-replaced.

"Listen," I said, "did you go and tell anybody that we were going to announce you as the grant winner? I was kind of hoping to keep it as a big surprise. There's members of the press here."

Ian shrugged. "Only a couple of folks, though they might have gone and told others. Didn't know it was an issue."

I'd never been able to deliver a proper penetrating gaze, and wasn't really built right for pinning someone against a wall until they confessed, so I just nodded a bit vaguely in response.

"Well, at least try to keep the lid on any chatter until I actually announce it," I handed him a pen, "which I'm not, until we get this all official."

He took the contract and pen, scanned over the former, signed it with the latter, and handed them back to me.

"This reminds me, I'm going to need you to sign some stuff before we start principal photography too. You have insurance on this place already?"

"I beg your pardon?"

He held his hands up, palms open, as though caught by a security guard. "Nothing serious, just standard forms we need for every location on which we shoot. Plus we're doing this on budget—got to keep costs down and work in some local color for cred."

"Ah. Well, alright, then. We'll handle that after. I think it's about our time out there."

We exited my office, and Ian went over to mill about with his people. I grabbed a cup and butter knife from the catering table and made my way to an area somewhat free of patrons, which happened to be in front of Verrick's painting. After attempting to clink the cup and knife together, which produced only a dull *twunk* sound since they were both made of plastic, I took a moment to compose myself, then cleared my throat loudly.

"If I may have your attention, folks."

They lent it to me, which was as terrifying as everybody says it is, though I'd always written them off because it's just people looking at you. I suddenly wondered if all the artworks secretly resented me for inflicting people's attention on them, but pushed the thought towards the back of my mind and realized I should probably stop just looking googly-eyed back at the crowd.

"Ah, thank you all, both regular patrons and newcomers alike, for coming out for our second annual Grant Gala." This was met with golf-applause. "I'd like to thank our first recipient, Myra Pavonine, for accomplishing so much with our first year's offering, several pieces of which you can find around you this evening. And it's without further hand-wringing that I'd like to announce the second recipient of our grant, chosen after a long period of deliberation from among a pool of talented applicants," I felt a little bad saying that, "and one whose accomplishments surely will elevate the Pioneer Valley along with him... Ian Irvin!"

This garnered more golf-claps from most of the audience, and some applause and whistling from one distinct sub-group as Ian made his way to the cleared area. I felt like I should have had an actual podium at which we would speak, but I merely stepped off to the side and worried at my sleeve as Ian took my place at the front of the crowd.

"Hey, guys" he began. "Glad you all made it out. I'm super psyched to be granted this honor, and I'm going to blow your expectations out of the water." He pantomimed an explosion with his hands. "You all know what I'm capable of with the accolades my first film, *The Fire that Refines Him*, received on the 'fest circuit, but I've got ambitions. Big visions. I'm looking to redefine the paradigm of the indie film scene... by creating the world's first indie action blockbuster right here in Treebridge using only the budget I'll receive from the Withers Art Trust."

Applause of the non-golf variety erupted from the audience. A handful of camera flashes went off. Though I had felt a bit dizzy at his unexpected announcement, I could definitely make out Decca in the crowd shouting, "ya fahkin' haahd-on," which was mostly buried under the crowd noise. Her Worcester accent slipping out was never a good sign. I didn't have time to run over and warn the caterers before Ian resumed speaking when the applause receded.

"It's not going to be easy, but it's going to be totally wicked. We're sourcing everything locally, getting the local culture involved, keeping it all with my peeps here in the Six Colleges. After all the exposure we get from this, Treebridge is going to become the next Toronto once Toronto becomes the next Seattle."

I didn't exactly get the last line, but the idea of getting Torontoer must have sounded impressive to the crowd, who responded with more applause.

"Booyah," Ian concluded. I elbowed my way back in front of him.

"So, ah, there you have it folks, oodles of excitement over the coming year! Go blog at him for more updates, but we really need to go dot the Ps and Qs on some legal hullabaloo before things get under way. Enjoy the refreshments while they last," I said to the crowd, then locked my arm in Ian's and edged us back towards my office. The applause stopped and was replaced by the sharp murmur of multiple groups talking to each other *over* each other about topics that my pulse was throbbing a little too hard in my ears for me to make out.

"Did you see how I lit the room up, man?" Ian asked me. Some people were making their way towards us from the crowd with eager looks in their eyes, and I felt then like I understood why all those Hollywood people have bouncers with them while out in public. The indie film world seemingly has yet to figure out a low-budget alternative to sternly-shaped men in suits. I can't imagine what it takes to feed one of those.

Fortunately, I was able to make it to the door before

anybody got within question-asking range, shoved Ian inside, and promptly shut the door on a boot, after which the rest of Decca followed us in. She stood in front of the door with the body language of someone approaching you in a dark alley, swinging a length of chain.

"Explain yahself and don't think I ain't packin' anythin' just 'cause I brought a clutch purse."

"How'd you get Fairuza Balk to accept an invite here?" Ian said with glee unbefitting the circumstance.

"This is Decca. She's half of the board of directors at the moment."

"Oh. What's the deal, then?"

"You said you wah gonna make a docu-frickin'-mennary."

"I'd agreed to make a *movie*, in writing," Ian said slowly, as though speaking to a child. "You've got my John Hitchcock right there on the dotted line. Nowhere in the contract did it say what *kind* of movie I was agreeing to make." He crossed his arms. "I had a moment of inspiration and it's gonna own bones."

Decca gave me a look that could have melted glass, then pointed at the contract sitting on my desk. Without making any sudden movements, I picked it up and handed it to her.

She skimmed it, and I was somewhat relieved that the pages didn't catch fire as she did. When she finished, she stepped aside from the door and leaned against the wall next to the jamb.

"He's right. There's nothing in there specifying the nature of the film on which he's to spend the grant, and he's already announced it to all creation out there. There's no way we can back down without losing face." Her voice had the sort of calm tension, which usually precedes a lamp hitting the wall. "We're funding his spectacle."

Ian let out a sigh of relief.

"Thanks, guys. I got this thing all planned out. Spec script, scouted a few set pieces, it's—"

"You can leave," said Decca.

"—all gonna go off without a hitch and blow people's fucking minds. Treebridge is gonna be THE—"

"You *should* leave," said Decca.

"You're right, there's hungry press out there waiting to get a hold of us. I know how to handle that sitch." He adjusted his lapels and made for the door. With his hand on the knob he opened it slightly and turned, pointing at Decca and myself with the pointer and pinkie of his free hand.

"I'll get back to you guys on those waivers. We're all in," he said, turning his hand up so he was giving us the horns, then slipped out. From the dark shape on the other side of the glass, I could tell that he stood in front of it with arms spread outwards for a moment, then blended in to the blur that was the rest of the crowd.

"We woulda been bettah off lettin' The K Foundation set the frickin' grant on fiah," Decca said, halfway to shouting. She tossed the contract towards my desk, where it landed with momentum that carried it off the far edge.

"I had no idea he was going to do that."

"Well ya dinn't—" she pinched the bridge of her nose for a moment, "—you didn't think to prevent something like that while drafting that damned thing." Decca helped herself to the chair on my side of the desk and picked up the contract.

"We could get a lawyer to advise us on the matter, maybe? You have to know somebody in the legal field; you've got priors."

"The only lawyer I know is a public defender in Holyoke and she's buried up to her neck in teens with dime bags planted on 'em. And if you back out—legally or otherwise—after a big announcement like that, you might as well start showing up to work in a Yankees cap for all the reputation you'll have at that point."

I shivered at the thought.

I remembered once at TSU, the morning after an important World Series game, finding the burned-out frames of several dorm couches on the quad arranged in the shape of the letter Y, enclosed by a circle of bent New York license plates the school later announced were harvested from the dorm parking lots. While I honestly can't recall whether the Sox had won or lost that game, Decca's meaning was quite clear: I'd get the art world equivalent of that.

"So what do we do about this?"

"You leave the office for a few minutes and I cool down without making a scene in front of people—then you ask me again."

I nodded and made my exit feeling, among several other uncomfortable things that needed time to percolate, relieved that I had a much-needed chance to grab the last of the evening's complimentary wine. The crowd in the gallery thinned, and I saw through our bay window that Ian gathered a sizable amount of it outside. With few people to maintain appearances around, I darted for the beverage station and grabbed a corked bottle of it-didn't-matter-what variety. Myra happened to be standing nearby, but she would understand a bit of ungentlemanly behavior.

"Greg," she said as I practically skidded to a halt, "I appreciate the attempt, but I don't really.... I don't know how well I came off."

"Pardon?" I said through the cork between my teeth, which probably came out closer to *pawwhum.*

"With Decca?"

"Oh, yeah." I held up a finger and took an urgent drink from the bottle to let her know there was a proper sentence to follow. "She has been pretty tense about things with the Foundation for the last week."

"And she did sorta just walk off when we were mid-conversation."

"She didn't leave or anything, there's just some people here that she doesn't really want to be around at the moment."

"Never mind," she snapped, then placed a hand on my forearm with a quick, small smile. "Sorry; you're a dear," she said in a softer tone, then grabbed another bottle of wine off of the table and slipped it into her purse. "Cheers!"

Myra turned and left, nudging politely through Ian's crowd at the door. That grave-mouthed gentleman bared his teeth pleasantly at her as she passed.

4

After the crowd dispersed, the caterers packed up, and we'd closed up the gallery for the evening, Decca and I held an impromptu board meeting at one of the three or four unaffiliated bars in the area named Finn MacCool's. I snagged a corner booth while she took a detour to the bar via the jukebox, then slid in carrying some kind of stout and a lighter beer topped with an orange.

"Damn baseball anthems are queued up," she said. "Girlier beer's yours, as usual."

"Much obliged. Do you happen to know how wine fits in with that beer-before-liquor adage?"

"I don't think the specifics matter at this point. We need to get our Cold Ducks all in a row."

We both drank to that.

"See," I said, "you're already joking around about things

again."

"That was just a reflex. There's still plenty to get pissy about. And I intend to." She idly stabbed her finger against the table like she was snuffing out a cigarette. "Fucking art-house action flick. He's going to put a boom mic through somebody's oil painting, or stuff Myra's copper coral full of squibs or something retaahded."

"I honestly had no idea Ian was going to pull something like that."

"That was a total theatre major move. Acting concentration, not stage tech; those guys are legit."

"We can just tear up the contract and say he never signed anything and not give him a cent. Nobody saw him do it. I was going to get it notarized just because important papers always seem to have one of those crimpy circles in the corner, but to hell with that."

"The contract stays in one piece, and don't do that anyways. Everybody there heard the announcement, and anybody who reads the local weekly for more than just concert listings is going to see it in a couple days. Probably earlier on the Internet," she leaned in close and took on a conspiratorial tone, "there are entire *messageboards* about the art scene here. Nonacademic theoretical discourse. Even the Society for Nonalterity and Strictarian Mimetic Representationalism are active—"

"Those words are just kind of college sounds to me."

"The Manifestians, for short. They're on there blogging and trying to shout people down. Stuff gets heated, reputations get made and ruined within a handful of pages, you don't even wanna know."

"I saw an argument they were having on one just the other day about that Verrick fellow. I think he actually responded."

Decca arched her eyebrows curiously. "Get out! You

don't seriously read them?"

"Only idly, while I'm waiting in line in the mornings. It was that coffee place at the bottom of the hill."

"You'll be better off if you just keep thinking we're talking about the same thing," she said with a smirk.

I shrugged and ate my garnish for lack of a meaningful response. I didn't see any real options on the table, either metaphorically or literally.

I imagined what a poster for Ian's film could look like. Somebody with a sloppy beard pedaling a bicycle away from an explosion rendered in orange and red crayon. A girl seated on the handlebars with some minor physical flaw like, a chipped incisor or port-wine stain that makes her seem more attainable for a guy with poor grooming habits. A letter or two in the title written backwards.

The only alternative was sending that gift horse straight in to the glue factory, with the caveat that Decca and I would be riding on it for the duration of the rendering process.

All we could do, it seemed, was make sure Ian didn't improvise anything else beyond the contract's language and try to ensure whatever film he did come up with wouldn't be something that would drag the Foundation through the mud along with it; or send shrapnel and extras flying through peoples canvases. My parents wouldn't mind funding a movie, but they'd certainly mind a bad movie that was theirs by proxy.

Sweet Caroline had been playing on the bar's stereo system, and Decca pantomimed a blowjob to the rhythm of the chorus, which succeeded in breaking my concentration.

"What'chu thinkin' 'bout, Withers?"

"We need to prevent this movie from becoming the laughingstock it sounds like it'll be. My parents would oust me for certain, and then where would I be with my American Studies degree? I'd have to settle for jobs that require a company-logoed polo shirt! You might have totally valid political objections to my lack of really doing anything for a living, but dammit, I just *like* a little feeling of status."

"Afraid they're going to cut off your trust fund?"

"I don't think I have one. It's not like we're rich-rich."

Decca *thonked* her glass on the table and gave me a wide-eyed, tilted-headed look. I'd seen it just often enough over the years to know that it was sign language for 'bitch, please.'

"You were able to front multiple cases of wine for a bunch of townies and reporters on the off-chance that they'd speak favorably of you."

"Australian wine," I said, defensively.

"Guess which class cares where wine comes from?"

"You know I don't know how to pronounce it." I slouched against the back of the booth, hoping I'd sink through its cushions and slip in to some kind of trippy Narnia-land where it was still impolite to talk about money with friends, and movie projectors hadn't been invented because there's never technology in those places.

"My poor *puh-TEET boo-schwa-SEE*. You don't know how to live, but you've got a lot of toys." She slid around to my side of the booth and punched me lightly on the arm. "Look, just because I advocate toppling your broad demographic doesn't mean I can't sympathize with your personal distresses. Besides, my reputation is entwined here and I'm not going to get the rug pulled out from under me by some chucklehead from Tarbox."

"Wait," I said, "but your family's from Lowell."

"Neighborly we ain't—I come from hardy Mill Girl stock. We used land along the river for means of production, instead of whatever the heck they have over in Essex County. Cut-rate universities where people too unsociable for even Brandeis wind up."

"Well regardless of where Ian's from, he's running free in Treebridge now and we need to try and corral him. He's gone mad with a relatively modest amount of budgeting power, and as a cannon he's loosening by the minute. Who knows what else he's going to decide to just up and change on a whim?"

"He didn't technically change anything on the bog standard contract template you used."

"He went back on his word to me," I said.

"Hell hath no slight peevishness like a Withers scorned, eh?"

"You jest now, but just wait until you see how badly I keep him in line. No line will have been kept within to such an extent as I'm about to keep his."

"Come again?"

"You heard me." I took a long sip of my fruity beer for dramatic emphasis.

"And what's the overall plan to accomplish this line-keeping? Just go on the defensive and react to whatever it is he comes up with? That means he's in control. We have to take the initiative. Go vanguard on his little special-snowflake operation."

I tried considering just how we might get the jump on Ian in this particular scenario, but I've never been one for problem solving. Besides, I was quite drunk. I fell back on reminiscing about an old Withers Furniture commercial where a family was repeatedly attacked by stop-motion animated couches and loveseats who were trying to devour their wallets and piggybanks, until a claymation version of my father swooped in and saved the day by pulling a budget-conscious Withers Reclining Sectional out of his wizard hat. I mean, it wasn't a direct analogy to our situation, and arguably magic doesn't exist, but I thought the basic principle still applied.

"We need a wizard hat."

"Greg, dear, you're babbling. I'm cutting you off."

I felt it was fair, as I realized then that my field of vision was sort of a Dutch angle regardless of how I held my head.

"I'll get him in to my office tomorrow and find out what

he's planning, and then we'll take his initiative," I said.

Just then, the Dropkick Murphys came up on the jukebox —causing Decca to shout, "Who put on the fuckin' plastic paddies?" as a reflex and after a heated exchange with several people all named Sully we were ejected from the bar. Which was probably for the best by that point of the evening.

Next morning... well, morning is a relative term after you wrap up an evening like I had.

The next afternoon, I opened the gallery and immediately got Ian on the phone, demanding that he come see me at his earliest convenience. He said he'd be over in a little while, which gave ibuprofen and coffee time to return me to a state in which I could command authority. I also took the time to call Myra, as I remembered something about her signing contracts with Ian as well. If I knew what he was already approved for, I figured I'd have a better idea of what I could and couldn't sign off on to keep his cannon-loosening to a minimum.

There was a telling pause between the phone being answered and Myra saying, "Nnnhello?"

"It sounds like you're another victim of whatever the hell tannins are."

"You always order the fucking Australianest wines for your openings."

I shrugged in response, not being in the sort of state where my body realized I wasn't having an in-person conversation. "They get the job done. Maybe a little too well. Anyways, you were saying something about insurance forms with Ian the other night. Do you remember exactly what it was that he had you sign?"

"Nnnrgh."

"Pardon?"

"That was a thinking noise. Necessary byproduct of such processes at this point of the morning."

Out of sympathy for her condition, I decided not to correct her idea of the timeframe.

"I'm pretty sure it was some all-encompassing release saying he can use moving pictures of me and my stuff as he sees fit, ipso facto terminus est, no deposit no return. That sort of deal."

"I see. No specific restrictions or anything?"

"I didn't read the whole thing before signing it, dude."

"Did he have it notarized?"

"I don't—what?"

"Just curious. Thanks for your help. Eat a banana!"

I hung up, finding myself in the same position I'd been in before the call, as far as making informed tactical decisions went. I devoured one of the bananas I'd brought for myself, and deposited the others in a desk drawer atop the rejected grant proposals. Nobody takes a man seriously with suggestive fruits on his desk.

Ian arrived after a period of time, which I wasn't really in a condition to keep track of. He knocked with a frustratingly cheerful shave-and-a-haircut rhythm, and I beckoned him in.

"Greggles, what's the haps?"

He oozed into the chair, and put his feet up on my desk. He was wearing a different blazer from the previous night, though it was still corduroy, and I felt a sudden resolve to never let the kind of person he was get the better of me.

I stopped trying to consciously suppress my hangover and let the physical annoyance work with me. *Be* the hangover, I decided. It was indirectly his fault after all.

"I believe we had some official business which we weren't able to get around to last night," I said.

"Ah yeah, the waivers." He produced a folded sheaf of papers from inside his blazer and smoothed them out on the desk.

"What exactly is this you need me to sign, again?"

"Just standard release papers. They just say that you agree to let me shoot on the premises here and I can use the footage for the movie."

"And what exactly are you going to be shooting here?"

"My movie, dude! What'd you get up to last—"

"Don't play coy with me, Ian." I wasn't expecting immediate results, but be was visibly uncoyed by my tone. I continued: "You know what I'm talking about. You were given this grant under the impression that you were just going to sit some people in the gallery and have them talk about it. Maybe a couple panning shots if you could fit it in to the budget. What the hell kind of stunt do you think you're trying to pull, and what kind of stunts are you hoping to film on my property around things I'm hoping to sell for a lot of money in their undamaged state? And do curb your Keds."

Ian's feet went floorwards, and he raised open hands in apology. I was considering conducting all of my official business with a hangover by that point. It was getting results even without holding a degree from UMass.

"Alright, I might have stepped all over your toes the other night. That's all on me. You're the boss. Totally should have run it by you. Mea culpa."

I clasped my hands together on the desk before me, and leaned slightly forward. I felt like I should have been graying at the temples and chewing on a cigar.

"So run it by me. I'm going to need to know exactly what you're doing well in advance of it getting done. That's the only way any of your skinnypants film crew are getting in to this gallery."

He slouched in his chair, produced a notebook from the

other side of his blazer and leafed through it haphazardly.

"Well, it's all still coming together."

"Start at the beginning. What's it called?"

"*Heisters.*"

I tried to adopt a withering gaze in spite of the dull pain around my eye area. With some effort, I succeeded in raising my bottom eyelids partway. Ian seemed to squirm ever so slightly.

"It's a working title," he said.

"Well, don't get rid of the flashy construction signs just yet. What's the plot?"

Ian leafed through his notebook again.

"So, it starts with this group of aimless twenty-somethings."

"Naturally." I didn't know I could sound so smug as a reflex, but Ian cringed. My head hurt less.

"So, uh, those guys are, like, upstart art thieves. Because you always see movies about those people getting the gang together for one last job, but like, they have to get their start somewhere, right? So they're just getting in to the whole art-thief scene, starting small, nothing really high stakes, but they still have to go and rappel down from air ducts and run from guys shooting at them. Because otherwise what's the point of an action blockbuster, right?"

"You want to shoot rope-climbing and gunfights in my gallery."

"Well, yeah, it's got all the stuff that the Heisters need to steal from the mafia."

"This is my career and reputation you're fucking with, realize."

"I'll fuck you not, buddy." He pulled yet another bundle of papers from inside his blazer. "We'll get you insured against any incidental damage during filming, and anyways, we won't actually have to do all that many stunts on location. Most of the explosions will be CG."

"What in the hell are you planning to explode? And where are you getting the budget for computer graphics, let alone insurance? You know exactly how much you're getting for this project."

At this, his confidence seemed to rebound a bit. I felt like I was getting out-maneuvered.

"I know a guy."

"You know a guy."

"He's a Hollywood accountant. He can work a little mathletics and make our spending add up to whatever we want it to look like on paper. Anybody who checks the books will see that it came in exactly on budget. Not to mention how many graphics guys you can find who're willing to work on a project like this just for the exposure."

I took a moment to process what was wrong with his proposition; aside from the ethics, where I wasn't really on any grounds to criticize.

"This isn't some minor matter of appearances. You aren't going to even have more than the initial grant money to budget with."

"I'll have plenty after I do a little local product placement."

I was able to muster a much blanker stare thus time, aided in part by the feeling that Decca would begin erasing me from old photographs if she were to hear about that.

"I know, dude, I know," Ian continued, "necessary evil in this day and age. I ran the numbers, and we can't get anything approaching a special effects budget with your grant, and none of us want this looking like some cheesy SyFy Channel schlockfest. This way we put out a good-looking product, and if anybody calls us on it, we can show them our Hollywood-accounted budget. Easy-peasy, lemon-squeezy." He made a juicing motion overtop his papers for emphasis, then pitched the imaginary rind towards my trashcan.

I had to admit, it helped sell me somewhat. Not on the wholesomeness of the idea, but on the possibility of just doing it and nobody would need to know. I'd already done that once by handing him the grant in the first place. Well, twice if you count the previous year. What was another minor moral compromise in the grand scheme of things if nobody had to know about it? What Decca didn't know wouldn't hurt me.

"How'd it go?" asked Decca. This was over the phone, in case I let slip anything that would make her reach for the nearest ice pick.

"It went well-ish. His initiative was lessened, if not stolen in its entirely, though perfidy did abound. There's significantly less initiative on his end than there was the other night, believe you me."

There was an uncomfortable pause.

"You get overly-wordy when you're nervous and skirting around something, just so you know. What happened?"

"Just residual nerves from the encounter. I held my own! He definitely won't be discombobulating much happenstance in the gallery. That's assuredly confirmed."

"Stop. Making. Your. Words. Fancy."
Her point was considered, and taken.

"We have the insurance stuff down in writing, in case anything does go awry."

"So he's still shooting an action movie with our money and doing it in the gallery, then."

"Most of the action will be shot off-site."

"Most."

"Yes, most."

"But not all?"

"Well, there'll need to be some scenes of the Heisters and the art in the same shot, but there's a lot they can do with just creative camera angles so that the gallery should remain—"

"Scenes of the what?"

"The gallery."

"No, the other word you used back there."

"Oh, um, that's just what the guys in the movie are called. They're D.I.Y. art thieves."

Each of the silences on her end seemed to be getting longer.

"It's at least vaguely topical, I'll give him that," came at last.

"I know, right? This might not be a complete call for existential doom and gloom."

"But there's still a fair amount of gloom potential, don't get all sunny-side-up just yet."

"Oh, you'll get no argument from me on that front. Gloom abounds."

"A surfeit of gloom."

"Gloom for one more."

"I'll high five the receiver for that one—but seriously, what's the practical plan for keeping this dude on a short kefiyeh?"

"Kefiyeh?"

"Those Middle-Eastern patterned scarves that clueless scenesters have been appropriating as of late."

"Appropriating?"

"Oh man, *seriously.* I hope you're just trying to dodge the original question with that. This won't look good to the rest of the Foundation come the quarterly evaluations."

"I... what? I don't think fellows conduct those."

"No they don't, but I think helping you outwit this indie twerp on short notice should get me a little more prestigious position than a mere fellowship, don't you?"

Ah, so the rub is laid.

"We can discuss that—"

"The specific title is up to your discretion, but I'm definitely working above my pay grade here. Pencil it in for whenever this thing wraps, no rush. But do use a pretty dark pencil."

I was being extorted, or blackmailed, or some other nefarious political term, that much I realized. But I was also desperately in need of the help I was being extorted for. So I guess that made it a win-win situation?

"Okay, okay... arch-fellow Decca—" there was some sort of chortle after that—"back to the original topic. I'm going to be present at all instances of filming, and whatever odd pre-film activities need to take place in or on the gallery, and ideally they'll need to run whatever they plan to do by me before it's allowed to happen."

Those damn pauses.

"Ideally."

"I mean, there's got to be some leeway for the creative spirit and epiphanies and what have you."

"I've written in Chris Hannah and Henry Rollins for every election since ninety-eight, I know from ideals. Don't give that opportunistic schmuck an inch. I put my trust in you as a fellow fellow."

"Fellow nothing, I'm the organization's head."

"Then you better not lead to us getting the shaft as well."

"Ew."

"Yeah, that was lowbrow, but this isn't going to be a clever day after the amount imbibed the previous night. I need to curl up with some Jeanette Winterson and work on not hurting. Let me know what else you plan to not let Ian do, whenever you figure that out."

Just as the call ended, I heard a suspiciously loud

crinkling sound coming from the front of the gallery. I peered around my office's doorframe to see a couple of people taping a swath of butcher paper to the storefront window.

I harnessed what I had left of the headache on my way to the front door and stormed, or at least blustered, outside to stare down the paperers. I assumed they were just naive art students who didn't understand that glass on the exterior of buildings often served a functional purpose, but I was greeted with something more worthy of my headache— Manifestians. The paper they were putting up read, in sloppy paintbrush-cursive, "*Ceci n'est pas une art.*" I had an advantage in their banner preventing them from seeing me approach, and proceeded to add their initiative to my collection for the day.

"What are you two stumpfuckers doing?" I asked, flecks of hangover-venom still on my tongue.

The two of them turned, letting one un-taped half of their banner droop free in the process. I recognized one of them from my previous soapbox encounter. His hair and beard were both shaved to the same length which, along with his fur-lined coat, had the effect of making him look like a particularly indignant plush toy.

"I'll have *you* know that we have a little thing called freedom of expression," he said, "and you're in no position—"

"I'm Greg Withers, owner and proprietor. That's my window that... that you're appropriating."

The second one seemed a little frightened by the word, but the first's eyes just got beadier in response, which furthered his stuffed animal impression.

"Don't you go leveling accusations to silence us, you pabulum-monger! We'll not tolerate your deprecation of high art through the elevation of intellectually-abstemious auteurs and promulgation of faux-cinematic dross!"

I set my feet and crossed my arms in response. Primarily because I had no idea what he was actually accusing me of, but also because the wind had just then gotten a hold of their loose banner and begun to carry it on a fluttering route down the street. The second Manifestian took notice and let out a sort of yipping cry, which alerted its papa bear to the escaping manifesto. He took off down the sidewalk after it, as the hairier one stared me down for a moment.

"Your aesthetic Philistinism will wither, Withers. You've awoken the sleeping giants on whose shoulders all artists stand!"

With that, he also took off after his impromptu kite. I stood there a moment wondering why they thought anybody here could even read Italian, then returned to my desk and bananas.

5

That Sunday morning, I woke to open the gallery doors at seven a.m. so Ian and his crew could begin principal photography. At eight thirty, his crew began to arrive piecemeal. Fortunately for me, the first crewmember to show up was the caterer, whom I recognized as the Quirky Best Friend from the coffee place I usually go to. Sticking to his word, Ian actually got a local business to provide the shoot with necessary caffeine, and probably-less-necessary muffins and tarts. I was glad he was making good on the promise of keeping his expenditures local, though after making some small talk with the barista while waiting for anybody else to show up, I asked if she happened to know how much they were being paid. She told me that Ian had said her shop would receive ample exposure in return for her services. I felt an imbalance in their agreement, but decided not to press the issue; since I was, at the moment, on the receiving end of said coffee and pastries. I dropped a dollar in her tip tar, hoping it would encourage others to follow suit.

Several other people filtered in over the next hour, and for the most part proceeded to mill about consuming coffee and mini-muffins. Part of me considered asking them to make sure they were there for the shoot and not just wandering in for the free food, but the uniform upscale-scrub appearance they all shared assured me that they were in the same circle of people Ian drew his usual crowds from. A handful of them were, in fact, carrying in spools of cable, standing lights, and scaffolding-type bits which they were setting down in what I could only assume were strategic locations throughout the gallery before helping themselves to coffee and leaving spare exposure in the barista's tip jar.

I wasn't exactly acquainted with anybody there, but since Ian was taking his sweet time showing up, I figured it would be in the Foundation's best interests if I performed some amateur reconnaissance on the crew members-in case they had any knowledge that might allow us to steal yet more of Ian's initiative. I didn't have a chance to shower before hoofing it downtown, which I figured was enough to let me approach them without raising suspicion. To top the impression off, I affected a look of mild boredom; which wasn't difficult, given the way that the morning had progressed.

I approached a group of crewmembers sitting on some hard plastic cases they'd stacked in the Vorticist nook. I greeted them with a friendly wave, which was met with quick upward head-nods. A brief silence ensued. Not an awkward one; a silence of social acceptance, or, at the very least, a resigned tolerance. Either way, I ventured a question while I still seemed to be on their good sides.

"So, what sort of scenes were you guys planning to shoot today?"

The one with the lopsided mustache responded. One of the ones with a lopsided mustache, rather.

"I dunno, man, we're just tech crew. We're bringing in what they've told us to and, whenever the boss man gets here, putting it where he says it goes."

I nodded. This was a new development. I'd sort of assumed that everybody involved with a movie had final copies of the script and knew exactly what was going on. Ian's approach to filmmaking was apparently similar to my approach to interfering with his filmmaking, which didn't bode well—because if I had no idea what I was doing, how was I supposed to have any idea what somebody else acting like me was doing?

I decided I should try and utilize a degree of logical deduction, and took stock of what the crew had been piling around the gallery. There were a bunch of hard plastic cases scattered around whose size and shape led me to wonder if they were carrying spare crewmembers. There was a pile of metal tubes and bars that looked like they were supposed to fit together. A pallet with a couple other pallets on top, which seemed oddly inefficient. There was also a pile of rope that caught my attention—that thin black professional sort of rope. It had several keychain clips fastened to it at points, and what looked like some kind of chest harness.

"Is that climbing gear?"

One of the other crewmembers responded.

"Yeah, Ian asked to borrow what I had. Rope, harness, pegs. Got to find an anchor point once Ian and the ladder get here."

"An anchor point."

"Yeah man. Rope isn't going to suspend itself."

I made a vague noise of acknowledgment since it wouldn't do any good to curse at them, then hurried back to my office. I called Ian again to no response, then texted Decca:

- *S.O.S. People want to screw things in to the gallery. Require assistance.*

Shortly after she texted back:

- I thought you didn't want to get screwed OUT OF the gallery? I have plans.

I racked my brain for an angle that would get her down here, and responded:

- Also caterer on set is devaluing their own labor.

Shortly after:

- Damn you. That's only going to work once, I'm not just some lefty Batman. On my way.

Feeling somewhat relieved that the cavalry was walking to the rescue, I returned to the gallery floor to check in on the crew again. A couple of them had begun knocking on the wall nearby to find studs, and the one who'd brought the climbing gear flagged me down as I approached.

"Hey, man, do you happen to have the blueprints for this place on hand?"

"I beg your pardon?"

"The blueprints for the building. We need to find the beams to drill in to."

I absolutely did not want the kind of people Ian could get to work for free to be jabbing things in to my walls or wielding hammers around friends' statues. Fortunately it was easy to stall them on that front even without lying.

"I don't actually know if we do or not. Tell you what, how about I go and see if they might not be kicking around in a filing cabinet somewhere, while you guys stand around and try not to put holes in anything?"

"Alright, but we're going to have to get moving on stuff once Ian gets here, we're already behind schedule."

"Have you heard from him?"

He shrugged. "Said he was on his way an hour ago."

I checked my cellphone. I'd still got nothing back from him.

"Well just run and grab me if he gets here before you start doing anything too structurally-integrative, OK?"

"Sure thing, man."

With that, I returned to my office and he wandered back towards the coffee station.

I didn't know if the gallery was the sort of place that needed blueprints. My folks chose the old storefront space due to the fact that it's just kind of a wide, empty shape with a couple of roof-supporting pillars scattered about. It seemed like everything you'd need to know about the building could be learned by just looking around and taking a couple of measurements. Since I hadn't the slightest idea where blueprints would be if they did exist, I decided to sit at my desk and take out the stack of rejected grant applications to look like I was actually doing something. I picked one out of the stack, which proposed filling an abandoned house in Springfield with plastic children's ball-pit balls, and hoped my eyebrows didn't betray my attempt at looking interested in it.

There was a knock on the doorframe, and I looked up to see Decca standing there. I motioned for her to enter. She tossed her messenger bag on to the chair and leaned over its back.

"What's the situation, chief?"

"Ian's got his people here planning to drill holes for climbing stuff in my gallery and I can't reach him to tell him to tell them to—"

"Yeah, no, I mean the caterer. Is that the only one out front there?

"Yes."

"Then I think I can solve both of our issues. Give me a few minutes to agitate and you just keep—" she looked at the stack of paper on my desk, "—ohh no, fuck that, read a book or something." She rooted around in her bag for a moment, and produced a brick-sized paperback that she tossed onto my desk —something with slums and wings on the cover. With that, she exited the office and I returned to looking preoccupied.

The thought occurred to me, as I was sitting there in front of a stack of bad ideas, that there was a nasty relationship between the quality of an artist's creations and the vigor with which they try to get said creations out there among the general populace. I mean, I thought of people like Chad, who to all observation seemed to put as much effort in to their actual art as I put in to my senior year, and how it kind of seemed like having some artistic accomplishment was almost a secondary concern; you just needed to slog through before you got to the real point of it, which was telling everybody how much of an artist you are. Their approach seemed more appropriate for someone silk-screening sloganed t-shirts than producing anything that could be broadly considered artistic.

Was I thinking the same thing as the Manifestians, but being less of a dick about it? They seemed to be simply opposed to anything that wasn't whatever they were doing. I think I was more opposed to art that didn't seem to have any purpose beyond drawing attention to the person that made it.

I flipped the stupid ball-pit application over and made a mental note to ask Decca if there was a more concise way to say what I think I thought. Shortly afterward, a chorus of groans from the gallery drew me out of my office again.

Amidst a crowd of disappointed folks in plaid shirts, the caterer packed her baked goods in to boxes. She slapped at the hand of one who tried reaching in for a parting danish.

"Hey," said the hand's owner, "we haven't even begun shooting! You can't go anywhere!"

"I can go somewhere that'll pay market rate for my services. You think this coffee just grows on trees? None of you fucking goofs were even tipping me."

There was a collective mumbling and shuffling of feet from the crowd. I noticed Decca leaning against a pillar off to the side, nonchalantly sipping a coffee of her own. Several of the crewmembers took out cellphones, and I had a feeling they were all texting the same person. Danish hand pointed at the caterer as she tipped her table over started collapsing the legs.

"Don't. We're going to straighten this out, just hang on."

The caterer rolled her eyes as she snapped the legs into place against the table's underside.

"Oh, what, you're going to feature my name *twice* in the movie's credits? Like anybody's going to sit through the tedious thing to see 'em anyways. Gimme a hand, Red?"

She and Decca picked up opposite ends of the table and carried it out the door. With the immediate cause of the problem out of sight, the crowd turned on me. I suppose I was the actual cause of the problem, but I don't see how they could have figured that out.

"What the fuck, man," one with a lumberjack's beard asked. He also had a lumberjack's upper body, so I was somewhat worried. I imagine I knew then what it felt like to knock over a row of motorcycles parked outside of a biker bar.

I raised my hands in front of me, palms open.

"Look, I don't have anything to do with the contracts you guys are using for crew, I can't force her to stay if she doesn't want to."

"But you're totally free to dismiss her if you're feeling a little whimsical?"

Decca and the caterer re-entered to carry some boxes of pastries and the giant coffee carafe out. Some of the group tried to get their attention as they left, to no end.

"Not doin' a shoot without coffee. No way," came from somewhere in the crowd, followed by two separate "this-is-bullshits."

"Get them to bring the food back in here, or today isn't happening," said the lumberjack.

"Why does this have anything to do with me? I'm not the one who decided not to pay the woman."

"Neither are we, we're just trying to fucking work here."

"She did have a tip jar."

"Are you trying to make something of it?" He crossed his arms in front of him. I worried his next line would suggest taking things outside, but fortunately Decca happened through the door just then.

"Just saw mister director pull up. Look alive, class traitors!"

The lumberjack gave me a sharp you're-gonna-get-it-now look, then turned to face the door. Decca fell into position next to me, and passed a paper bag that felt like it contained baked goods behind our backs, whispering, "the spoils of solidarity."

Ian entered, along with a small group of his people, and surveyed the scene. Everybody immediately fell silent, like a classroom when the teacher had just walked in.

"Someone tell me why my phone's ringtone has been on a permanent loop for the last five minutes," he asked.

"I've been waiting for hours for you guys to start filming and now you're planning on drilling holes in to my walls?" I asked—at the same time that Lumberjack said, "Riot Grrrl made the caterer pack up and leave, and Trustfund is trying to reneg on the set piece."

"One at a time, dudes," Ian said.

"The caterer decided that her services were being undervalued and left to pursue more profitable ventures," Decca interjected before the Lumberjack could speak. "You can probably just ask her to return your exposure to you if you paid it in advance."

Ian studied her for a moment, then said, "You're the manic pixie chick from the other night?"

"Yep! And still packin'."

Ian regarded her blankly for another second, then turned to the assembled crew and took out his cellphone.

"Alright, give me a headcount. I'm ordering pizza on my

dime for all of you guys so we can get this thing off the ground. Now get to assembling!"

There was a chorus of happy noises from the crew, and they separated in to smaller groups around the gallery space, putting together all the things they'd brought in and sat on for the previous hours. Ian pointed at me and said, "Let me get things rolling here then we'll hash all of this out," then began making his way around to the different groups, giving them hasty instructions while gesturing with his hands, seeming like a maestro moving among several small, under-dressed orchestras.

"I'm surprised they found a brand of skinny jeans durable enough to wear for manual labor," Decca said, as she pointed to a particularly fashionable crewmember making a half-hearted attempt at lifting from the knees.

I was somewhat impressed with the speed at which things were coming together now that Ian had given the order (both in the commanding sense and the pizza sense,) though I was still a bit worried by the sheer amounts of scaffolding getting bolted together in one corner of the gallery. It was sort of a tripod up to about five feet, then extended one shaft up nearly to the ceiling where it split off in to a T shape.

"What do you think that's supposed to be for?" I asked Decca.

"No idea."

"I really don't think I trust probably-unpaid guys to keep that thing upright for any amount of time."

I didn't wait for her to respond, something about actually voicing the concern seemed to create a sense of motivation in me. I went over to Ian, who at that point was sitting on a bench with the Newsie from Thursday. "—then you just stop and suddenly look wistful," Ian was saying, "wicked fuckin' wistful. Because the painting reminds you of your high school girlfriend, see?"

I wasn't quite sure how to interrupt someone in a professional manner, so I cleared my throat rather loudly. They looked up at me.

"I don't know what the heck you're planning to do here today but I'm really not comfortable with your crew trying to punch holes in my walls and it looks like you're preparing to hang a giant man over there," I said, perhaps too quickly. My face felt warm.

Ian handed the script to the Newsie.

"Go outside for ten, look it over, do your Method thing and get psyched, OK?"

Newsie did so, giving me one of the sidelongest glances I think I've ever gotten on his way past me. Then Ian motioned towards the vacated side of the bench. I sat.

"Look, bro," he said, "I know I haven't been as clear as I should've been about what's going on, and that's all on me. I'll own up to that. But I'm going, like, domino epiphanies with this, and my guys are just trying to figure out how to do what I've been saying we should when I'm not around to instruct them."

"You're supposed to run *everything* by me before you take any kind of action here."

"I know that, man, but the ideas are just coming too fast and furious to keep you in the loop. As soon as I say something and get my team on it, boom, better idea comes along and drowns that last baby in its bathwater." I imagine I made a sour face at that expression, but it didn't deter him if I did. "If I were keeping you up to date with every little development, I'd burn through all your anytime minutes."

"Well, thanks, I guess. But whatever you're looking to do here today, I really don't like the look of this equipment you're putting together. To say nothing of what you want to do to the walls."

He cupped his chin in his hand; the universally acknowledged sign that one was thinking, then looked at the hangman thing the crew had set up and nodded. "We can do it without the holes in the ceiling if that's what's eating you, no problem."

"Ceiling?"

"Hey Darren!"

Somebody ascending a ladder near one of my pillars stopped and turned—the Lumberjack, actually.

"No securing anything to the actual building. We'll do it all from the scaffolds and scrub it out in post."

"Seriously?" Lumberjack shouted across the gallery.

"Seriously."

Lumberjack gave an exaggerated shrug and began descending the ladder.

"That's the other thing," I said, "I don't... I mean, you're going to have people swinging around on ropes in here?"

"Yeah dude, the Heisters need to break through the skylight and rappel down to get in to the place."

"We don't have a skylight."

"You will in post, trust me. But they're going to be going straight up and down on that thing," Ian gestured towards the hangman, "no swinging around and going out of control, nothing dangerous. I got your back on this."

"Well, that is reassuring—"

I was interrupted by someone shouting, "You may be dismayed to learn your production has been infiltrated," nearby. Lumberjack and two other crewmembers folded their ladder and, taking hold in the middle and on each end, began carrying it towards the door. The person in the lead, however, had let go of the ladder to shout that. He pulled at his distressed jeans, which tore away to reveal conservative pleated slacks, and ripped open his gaudy plaid button-up to show a solid-color dress shirt and tie. At his signal, several similarly dressed individuals stormed into the gallery, carrying meticulously lettered signs that read, "WE OPPOSE THIS OSTENTATIOUS

72

DERELICTION OF ARTISTIC PRINCIPLE." One sign had what I think was supposed to be a caricature of Ian holding a film reel which had dollar signs in the individual cells, along with a word bubble saying, "Why yes, there is no business like show business ha ha." I recognized the one who used the same clipper setting on both his beard and his hair. He was carrying a manifesto, from which he began to read.

"Let it be publicly acknowledged heretofore that there does exist within Treebridge significant aesthetic opposition..."

He continued on. I noticed that Decca was leaning against a column halfway between us and the group. When she saw me looking at her, she held a fist to the side of her face and sign-languaged fellatio again, poking her tongue into her cheek.

"Who the fuck are these guys? Are they with that *But I'm A Cheerleader* friend of yours?" Ian asked. He was laughing, but it was that not-actually-amused Jack Nicholson sort of laughter.

"Decca and I are not at all connected with them. They're a local group of art... well, if there's a word that means the opposite of enthusiast, I guess that's what they'd be."

Ian stood, cupped his hands around his mouth and shouted, "Hey, fuck-o, this is a live set!"

The head Manifestian stopped reading.

"I'm filmin' here! Shoot in progress! Get the fuck out!"

Some of the Manifestians exchanged nervous glances. The leader flipped a couple pages ahead in his manifesto and continued reading at a quicker pace.

"Um, it is therefore deemed appropriate and in thorough good conscience to forewarn innocent passersby of the falsely-advertised bread-and-circus," at this, several of them pulled large stickers out of their pockets that said DEEMED BY COMMITTEE NOT TO BE ART and began to pull the backing strips off. "This action to be commenced immediately upon dispersion of our official missive!"

The sticker-wielders then slapped them on the nearest

surface at the conclusion of the manifesto, whether it was a wall or a window or the side of a podium. Fortunately, they happened to avoid stickering any actual artworks. They then spread out, drawing more stickers as they did so.

"Motherfuck," Ian and I said in near unison.

"Guys, stop them from messing up the goddamn set," Ian said, while I just stood there, mouth agape. Crew members began an awkward football-interception dance with the stickerers, moving around and trying to cut them off from any flat surfaces without actually touching them or getting in to a physical altercation. The head Manifestian holstered his papers, drew a sticker of his own, and made a beeline for Ian and I; only to trip over the boot Decca stuck into his path.

I noticed that the original infiltrator was trying to tag his former ladder-carrying partners. He'd jab the sticker forward, and they'd step back and raise the ladder horizontally in front of themselves. After a few such feints, Lumberjack turned the ladder and thrust it forward, to try and push the infiltrator further away. He grabbed onto a rung and tried pulling it, but had neither the beard, nor the stature, to win a contest of strength against someone nicknamed "Lumberjack." The crew yanked the ladder back forcefully, pulling the Manifestian off his feet and sending the other end of the ladder into the podium that held Myra's "Memories Dull My Senses."

The force of the blow sent the jaggedy-cat-thing airborne, and it flew quite a bit further than I would have thought something shaped like that could. Its shape also proved beneficial to puncturing the canvas of the large Verrick painting it eventually hit. Not to the painting's benefit, I mean; that wound up tearing open and being knocked loose from its hanging wires, and hit the floor hard enough that one of the frame's bottom corners split apart. It flopped against the wall and leaned there like a boxer catching a breather against the ropes. Myra's statue skittered to a halt nearby, somehow still intact.

I'd presume time passed between that happening and somebody saying something, but I honestly couldn't begin to estimate the actual time elapsed. I also didn't know if the sun actually turned red, or if it was only my vision being affected. Fortunately, one of Ian's crew broke the silence to let time happen again.

"Wasn't me."

"Fuck, dude, I didn't touch that," said the headlong Manifestian.

"You were provoking me, you little shit. I was in total fight or flight mode," Lumberjack said.

I noticed Ian edging towards me out of the side of my vision, but I was still focused on the ruins.

"Look, Greg, we'll adjourn for the day, and tomorrow we'll—"

He put a hand on my shoulder. I just said, "Out. Everybody," in as calm a voice as I could, and that seemed to be all the prompt anybody needed at that point. The Manifestians and most of Ian's crew made an immediate break for the door, though some of the crew hesitated, glancing nervously around at their equipment.

"We'll get it tomorrow, guys," Ian said. "This isn't Jason Schwartzman pitching a hissy again, somebody's liable here."

I watched them all leave, then turned to Ian.

"Dude, I'm totally sorry that—"

"Tomorrow morning," I said, practically able to feel the icicles hanging from the words as I spoke. "Be here when we open. Things are getting renegotiated."

"Gotcha. My apologies." He made a hasty retreat, leaving me and Decca in the gallery.

I leaned back against the wall and slid down to a sitting position on the floor. My face felt like it was paler than all of Alpha Delta Phi. Decca gingerly approached.

"I'm not even going to pretend that I know what's going through your head right now. Just tell me if you need someone here, or if you want solitude."

I considered this.

"I think I need to be alone right now, but I need you here tomorrow morning. For support, and as verbal muscle."

"I'll pick you up at ten. Hey," she put a hand on my shoulder, "this'll get fixed somehow. Chin up, tow-head." Then she split.

I sat there, bogged down with a feeling of disgust at the sight of the broken painting leaning there. After some amount of time, willed myself to my feet. I shut the lights off and drew the curtains across the bay window. I stepped out of the gallery and, as I was locking the front door, a car pulled up outside. The driver got out of it and asked me what the address of the building was. I told him. He was wearing a T-shirt with a logo on the chest that was a pizza topped with pepperoni and shamrocks, and I thought I recognized him as someone whose paintings I'd had on display at some point.

"I've got an order of eight larges for this place," he said. "Name on the card is Withers?"

6

After a breakfast of cold Mickey Marinara's (the first of about fifteen, I estimated, courtesy of Ian,) Decca picked me up at my apartment. She even went so far as to sweep a layer of 'zines off of her passenger seat for me.

She handed me a coffee as I got in. "Courtesy of our newly class-conscious cafe."

"How're you holding up?" she said.

"Well enough, I suppose, for somebody who might be looking down the barrel of a couple lawsuits from his artists."

"Your contracts don't actually say that you're culpable for any damages incurred, do they?"

"I have *no* idea, that's the problem. You've seen the amount of useless sentences they put in those things."

She gave a slow, thoughtful nod.

"Well, Myra's a friend of yours. She'd probably let you off just settling out of court; even if she is the rare artist who can afford a lawyer."

"Well, we'll find out. I told her about it last night and asked her to meet us there too."

"How'd she sound?"

"It was over text, so... she didn't. Her response was just, 'Okay, seeya there.'"

"Cryptic! What about the guy with the painting?"

"I haven't even tried to get in touch with him. He's a recluse, and it's probably pretty expensive to be one of those since you need a good amount of land to fence off and hire some butlers, so he might be able to send a mob of litigators after me."

"Those reclusive types tend to be a little insane, too, so there's that to factor in."

"I am going to so much jail."

"Affluent white dude in a college town? You'll be fine."

"At the very least, my parents will disown me once they find out. No more gallery, no foundation, no career. I'd be lucky to be handed a sympathetic sales position at the Withers Furniture Factory Outlet in Monson."

"Monson would eat you alive! You think dealing with the yuppies up here is taxing, that's hill-folk country. Like a little chunk of New Hampshire that couldn't cut it up there and sought shelter in bluer climes."

The line of conversation wasn't all that reassuring. Fortunately, it was interrupted from a text from Myra:

- The lights are on but nobody's home.

"What do you make of this now?" I held the phone to face her.

"Driving!"

"Ah. Right." We weren't far from the gallery at that point, so I figured it would be explained soon enough. I examined one of the 'zines on the floor in front of my seat, *Expose the Culprits and Feed 'Em to the Children.* It was one of hers.

"You're still putting out stuff as Alice Alter even after making it to the big time?"

She gave me a crooked smile.

"You flatter me; two part-time gigs at two out of the Six Colleges is hardly topping the academic heap. And the spiritual rewards there are... minimal."

"But you have the book out."

"It's just critical essays put out by a university press that say things about aesthetics, and the academy; that people in the upper echelons of said academy don't like to hear, so all that really gets me is the occasional guest column in *Bitch Magazine* and a Christmas card from Samuel Delany. Putting out polemical poetry on the Business School's copier after hours keeps me from retreating entirely within the ivory tower and ceasing to care about matters that aren't wholly theoretical."

I'd known *of* Decca for maybe a year or so before I actually came to know her. Alice Alter 'zines were appearing in local bookstores, tucked in napkin holders at coffee shops, and in small piles around the Six Colleges' campuses since the early aughts. They were all a single sheet—cut and folded into eight pages; sometimes illustrated, sometimes just blank verse song lyric-y poetry, but usually addressing specific political matters like Springfield's Financial Control Board, or the redrawing of state park boundaries between the Quabbin Reservoir and Miskatonic River.

"You've been doing this for what, seven or eight years now? You must have a huge backlog of material built up. You could do something, I dunno, official with it."

"Few enough publishers will pay an advance for poetry manuscripts nowadays. Adding overt politics in to the mix? Nah. I'm not looking to change a system from within. If I'm doing it for free, I'm doing it the traditional Trotskyist way— sloppily Xeroxed and forced on strangers. And honestly, I'm a little too proud to want word to get out that I'm an *aspiring artist.*" She paused to roll her side window down and shout "GREEN!" at the car ahead of us. "So, are you inviting the Manifestians to our meeting? They could easily be co-defendants."

"I wouldn't have the first idea of how to get in touch with them."

"I think you just have to say 'comic books being taught as literature' in to a bathroom mirror three times after dark, then they'll appear behind you."

"I knew I was hosting this meeting too early."

We pulled in to the public lot down the block from the gallery and proceeded to walk over. Myra was already standing out front. She waved enthusiastically when she saw us approaching.

"You left the lights on, goof," she called to us.

We got to the window and I noticed through the curtains, that there were indeed lights on inside the gallery. Apparently purple ones, which weren't something I'd ever had installed.

"I definitely turned them out when I left last night."

"Maybe some Smithies broke in to host a late-night flashmob rave," Decca said.

I pulled at the door, which was still locked. I took my keys out, opened it, and pushed the doorstop in to place.

"You don't know if it's safe to go in there," said Myra, "someone might still be inside."

"Nobody could have gotten inside, this is the only door in to the place and the windows aren't busted."

"I *am* still packing, y'know," Decca said.

"To an art gallery?" said Myra.

"By all means," I said, and gestured through the open door.

Decca slid some sort of black handle from within her boot and tucked it into her front pocket. She peered around the jamb briefly, then stepped inside. I followed, with Myra behind me.

The track lights running along the ceiling definitely hadn't been left on, which wasn't much relief given the rest of the scene. Instead, the purple glow seemed to be emanating from the wall behind the tattered ruins of the painting. It was... not ultraviolet, since I don't think that's actually visible to humans, but it was somehow the most purple thing I'd seen outside of that Creative Nonfiction course I took as an elective.

"I hope I shouldn't have brought a Geiger counter instead of a baton," said Decca.

The light flickered at the sound of her voice, then grew brighter. Each of us shouted a different curse word in response to it. It then flared even brighter and I ran to the fire alarm, grasped the handle, and tore its papier-mâché housing clean off the wall.

Decca was too focused on the bizarre light to take notice, but Myra turned at the sound. Her shocked mouth developed an upward curve at the edges once she realized what had happened.

"Oh damn it, if this gallery doesn't totally burn down then No. More. Installation. Art," I said, then dropped the false fire alarm to take out my phone and dial 911. Then I dropped that too, because an enormous, dark green arm emerged from behind the painting.

Seriously.

Myra screamed and ran into my office. Decca backed away from it, coming up against a pillar, then shuffled behind it.

It grabbed on to the broken frame with webbed fingers and tensed, pulling the frame down and slapping against the floor in an awkward motion that seemed unintentional. I heard Myra scream from within my office at the impact, which was like an enormous pile of Yankees fans' wet clothes thrown from a dorm window. Decca slumped down against the pillar and clutched her arms tightly around her torso, breathing rapidly. She looked at me, standing there in the open with nothing but a probably-broken phone on the floor between me and the thing that was happening, then leaned around the pillar to look for herself.

The frame falling had revealed that the arm was emerging from a large extrapurple® glowing spot that looked like it had been smeared around a point where the floor and wall met, through which another set of webbed fingers emerged and flattened against the wall. The first arm turned palm-down on the floor, braced itself, and pulled the rest of itself out. An enormous ridge of dark shell crested out from the spreading extrapurple® area between the two hands, accompanied by a bizarre atonal flute-noise, and anything that may have followed that hopefully wasn't worth standing around for, as I'd already turned and ran for the front door.

I stopped after crossing the gallery threshold to make a grab for the door and Decca slammed in to me, knocking me on my ass on the sidewalk. She stopped in the doorway to look back, noticed Myra wasn't following, then grabbed me by the forearm and pulled me back up. I shoved the doorstop aside with my foot and the door swung closed, for whatever good that might do.

"So, we have at least one reason to go back in there. Fuck," said Decca. She kicked at the doorstop, which just clattered hollowly on the pavement.

I looked up and down the street. There were people wandering around, and somebody playing a handsaw with a violin's bow across the street. Fortunately, we hadn't drawn any undue attention from the outside; though I suppose any amount of attention paid to the arrival of giant monsters would actually be very due.

"I don't want to get eaten by that thing," I rasped.

"Neither do I."

"I definitely don't want to be responsible for Myra getting eaten by that thing."

"Ditto."

We looked at each other for a moment. She looked towards the gallery door.

"So, are we doing this?" she asked.

I took a deep breath, and before I could respond, she yanked the door back open with one arm, grabbed my arm with her other, then both pulled us inside and the door closed behind us with one quick turning motion.

It took a moment for my eyes to reorient to the dim purpleness inside the gallery after being outside at mid-day. I could definitely see through my open office door. Myra was crouched under my desk with her hands over her head, like a tornado drill at school. I think I heard a faint, continuous muttering coming from her.

The thing from the painting was still in the main hall, apparently done dragging itself forth. What I suppose was its upper body was jutting out from the now-larger purple shimmer on the wall, propping itself up on two large arms. Two smaller clawed appendages were folded against the front of its chest, or maybe its underbelly—I couldn't say that for certain since it didn't have a head or face to serve as a reference, just a mass of tentacles that seemed to be floating upright like seaweed; swaying slightly though no breeze was present in the gallery and I was reasonably certain that we were not under water. The whole of the thing was a dull dark green, somewhat lighter and shinier at the parts where sections of the shell covering the core of its body came together in ridges.

It seemed rather ineffectually designed for whatever it was actually supposed to do.

Decca *pssted* at Myra, trying to get her attention. The creature's kelp-like head-analogue swayed at the noise, and it angled its body to face the two of us.

"Esteemed mortals! I have arrived through long-barred means and do extend my gratitude to you as the way's openers and de facto ambassadors," it said, in a voice that was both glottal and singsong. I couldn't see where a mouth might be on it; I presumed it was somewhere buried beneath the headkelp.

Decca looked at me, pointed at it, and mouthed something I couldn't decipher but which definitely had the word *you* in it.

I took a few hesitant steps towards the thing and, not really having any idea what the standard of conduct was for greeting whatever it was, waved.

"Hello... sir?"

"And what would your name be, he who heralds my unfolding planewards to those perceived by your limited faculties?"

"I'm Greg Withers. This is my fellow, Decca Lyne."

It shifted its weight to the side and leaned on the elbow of its left humanoid arm. The noise of it shocked Myra into screaming again. It splayed one of its torso-claws in a gesture that seemed to return my wave.

"Greetings, Gregwithers and Deccalyne! I am Tzmirtalhuanchnivaalnimrtchuul."

"That's—I'm sorry, but that's going to be a bit difficult for us to pronounce."

"I understand your limited sonic capacity."

"Do you mind if we just call you Tzmir, or something?"

"Indeed I do."

"Um, alright." I worried at my sleeve for a moment, unsure of how to proceed tactfully around whatever Tzmir was. "So can I ask why you've decided to come here?"

"As linear time follows the curves of the universal planes, so too must I travel by means of its interstices."

I looked towards Decca since she spoke fluent Academese.

84

She shrugged. "It has to move through corners? In space and maybe time?"

"These are truths," it said.

I addressed Tzmir again. "That explains why you're here in that very specific part of the wall, but I mean why did you decide to arrive in my art gallery? Are you under the impression that we called you forth or something?"

Its headkelp shivered and fanned out briefly, then returned to their regular wafting state.

"I had been hailed to these planes by a priorly-enacted sigil, the route to which was then cut off, and which has recently been opened. I presume that was your doing. And by your tone of inquiry I'm led to conclude that you two would not be the architects of the original sigil?"

I shook my head quite firmly.

Decca called over to my office: "Myra, have you been drawing any sigils? Or building them? Whatever it is you do to make one?"

She didn't respond.

"Then I manifest unbound," Tzmir said. It rose back up to its original posture, arched its back and fanned its headkelp out.

"That doesn't sound good," Decca whispered to me.

"I do appear to have unfolded amidst a site dedicated to aesthetic ebullience. As I have arrived, so shall I proceed!" It raised a finger before it, as though it had just made a point, and mimicked the gesture with a claw on the same side. "Fortunate, if not an outright display of ultra-terrestrial providence, as in matters of artistic self-expression, you might say that I have a special plan for this world."

"I'm sorry," I said, "you're... what are you doing?"

"It sounds like it's invading," said Decca.

"SON OF A BITCH BASTARD WHORE," came from my office and continued in that fashion until it winnowed down into a despairing wail.

Tzmir emitted what, in context, must have been an attempt at a scoff. "Everyone's a critic. Who are you to deride my art, simply because I choose to limit its form to three spatial dimensions? I may not craft such intricate progeny-manifold displays as Shub-Nigurath, sure, but I'm entirely self-taught!"

There was an awkward pause, then Decca said, "I take that back, you're being solicited."

"I present not solicitation but an edict!" Tzmir pointed a finger and a claw at the floor for emphasis. "Let this gallery serve as the original manifestation of my manifesto."

I hadn't needed to hear that word again. "This has to be some joke it plays, so it can devour happy prey," to Decca. Tzmir continued without seeming to hear, however it managed to hear things without visible ears.

"The true art in asking is to phrase desire as statement, and you three, if you don't mind, shall serve to inform the greater populace."

A small group of Tzmir's headkelp twisted around each other to form a more substantial tentacle that stretched down the length of the wall towards my office. There was another scream from within and Myra emerged, swatting at a strand that seemed like it was trying to get a hold of her. She ran over, either tripping or collapsing as she reached us and sat with her knees pulled up to her chest. The tentacle withdrew from my office carrying a sheaf of paper.

I was really coming to dread the sight of people brandishing any amount of paper in front of me after the last couple of days.

Tzmir brought the papers back to the main mass of its headkelp and circulated bunches among the individual strands, passing them back and forth. They each seemed to be three or four sheets stapled together.

Decca prodded me in the shoulder.

"Those aren't what they look like they are, are they?"

"Huzzah," said Tzmir, "Let my manifestation be heralded by the conversion of an abandoned house in to a festive ball pit! Squalor to be masked by merriment! The lower orders shall come to appreciate my pan-dimensional vision in time."

"Oh my Goddess," said Decca.

Tzmir paused in its motions and... it didn't have eyes, but I got the feeling it was regarding us with a raised brow.

"Have you not acknowledged this conceptual tour-de-force outlined within your very own gallery? Permit me to expound its virtues. And I quote," Tzmir transferred one packet of papers to its front claws, held it up towards its headkelp, and cleared what must have been a throat. "Call this an interactive art installation, a neighborhood development initiative, or just totally crazy, but there'll be a glimmer of hope in this giant ball pit. It's silly, I know, but it's serious too! There's really important work to do to bring attention to these dangerous abandoned properties and turn them in to something worthwhile..."

Decca began laughing when Tzmir started reading, but just then she clapped her hands over her ears, turned on a heel and started walking to the door singing something up-tempo in a snotty voice to drown it out.

I didn't exactly blame her for doing so, but I stayed. Partially out of a feeling of responsibility, since it was my gallery this thing had appeared in and it hadn't really explained why or who had actually brought it here. I guess the how of it had been covered, though not really with words that meant something to people. It was also my grant contest that he seemed to be hijacking.

Tzmir finished reading, and its body language implied it was looking expectantly at us.

"Isn't that just the coolest?" Tzmir said.

I knelt down to pull Myra to her feet. She muttered,

"They've been invisible but they could see us. They remain in shadows growing wings, wakeful wry and watchful they await deathless," as I was helping her up. I didn't know what to make of that, so I addressed Tzmir again.

"I'm glad that you like the proposals there, but that's our reject pile. We aren't funding those."

Tzmir moved an enormous hand to where its neck might have been, seeking pearls to clutch.

"An aesthetic curator would deny such whimsy?"

"Well... I suppose there is some human truth in it."

"Limit not your terms of praise by genus nor phylum, this eminent brilliance must be enacted! Once my subordinates arrive, we'll begin with this assuredly artistic endeavor. Until then, Gregwithers and crying friend, I recommend you go forth and herald my arrival! Report back and tell me of the news' reception. Go! On with you!" It followed that by flicking Myra's fallen statue at us like a paper football with one of its giant fingers. The jagged thing skittered across the floor to our feet, where Myra picked it up. I put my arm around her and we turned and left as Tzmir emitted that unearthly flute noise from within its lack-of-a-head again.

Outside, Decca had managed to intercept a fashionably-late Ian. Judging by the look on his face, he'd heard the weird call that Tzmir had just made.

"So I can't go in because you're banging an elephant?" he said.

"I was trying to not tell him about—y'know," said Decca.

I took my arm off of Myra after seeing she could stand on her own, and locked the door. The blinds were fortunately still down from the previous day.

"Something, um, has come up," I said.

"I don't think that direction is meaningful to it," said Myra.

"If this is about culpability for the damages, I've got

waivers galore right here." Ian's hand made for the inside of his jacket, and I held out a hand to stop him.

"Dammit, no, no more papers. Not now."

"We should probably go somewhere to talk about this," said Decca. "Ian, there's something we might be accessory to that small print doesn't typically cover."

He looked at the two of us, then at Myra, who was just gazing at the sidewalk with a vacant look in her eyes, clutching her spiky cat statue. Her distraught state seemed to key him in to something serious being afoot.

"Alright," he said, "let's do lunch."

We huddled in a booth at Woostah Sauce, a pub adjacent to the TSU campus, on the hunch that anybody there on a Monday afternoon would be too busy nursing a hangover to care about overhearing somebody else's conversation. Decca borrowed a ten to put the Distillers' entire discography on the jukebox for further cover. Myra seemed to have recovered somewhat on the walk over, to the point where she was speaking in more than cryptic mutterings and could meet people's eyes. She sat next to Ian, across from Decca and myself.

"I'm not really sure where to start with this," I said.

"There's a giant alien in the gallery who says that we somehow called it up during that skirmish yesterday," said Decca.

Ian appeared, understandably, unreceptive to the idea.

"I know it looks like I've been trying to pull a bunch of fast ones on you guys, but if you're trying to goose my gander here, really, don't go for the sci-fi. Magical realism, at most."

Decca propped her head up on an arm, elbow on the table.

"Based on our few interactions so far, do I seem like the kind of person who'd try to mess with your head instead of just slashing your tires and stealing your girlfriend?"

"Ian, you heard it in the gallery when we were there," I said.

"Show it to me, then."

"I didn't really think that would have been the safest course of action without you knowing what you were getting in to. It seems like it can inflict slight fits of insanity on people. You okay, Myra?"

She nodded slowly. "I'm just trying to process it all—the scope of it. I mean, yeah I've read pulpy stories about this kind of thing, but that's all secret cults in dank basements who call these things up. This was... did my art bring it here? Am I responsible for that thing?"

"We don't know that," I said.

"Your statue did fly through that painting and hit the wall where the thing is," said Decca. "But it was wicked evasive when it was explaining things. Could have been that anything piercing the wall at the right angle would have done it."

"It means something that my statue was involved and it tried reaching for me."

"I think it was just grabbing for the papers you were close to," said Decca.

"It's not coincidence. I don't know why I ran in to that room. It's significant."

"Hey, now. Lip Ring, Gypsy Skirt, back it up a bit," said Ian. "Give me the downlow on what's going on. Walk me through."

"I have a name," said Myra.

Conversation halted as the waiter arrived with four mugs of coffee and a couple tiny milk pitchers. Ian emptied most of one of them in to his mug.

"Take your coffee how you take the racial makeup of

your casts?" said Decca.

"The fuck does that even mean? You zooin' on me?"

"Ya wanna go?" Decca held her arms out to the sides and sized Ian up like he were a folding table.

I slapped an open hand down on to the tabletop.

"Can we drop the standoffishness? Nobody's suing anybody else and nobody knows what the hell started this whole thing and even if we aren't directly responsible, we're absolutely going to look like it when word gets out that there's a giant.... headless.... some kind of whistling man-armed squidlobster sitting in my gallery."

Decca, Ian, and Myra looked at each other briefly.

"You're right," said Ian, "if that gets out, we're all screwed."

"We might be screwed regardless of whether or not word gets out, that thing said it's bringing other things," said Myra.

"We don't know why it's bringing other things," I said.

"When is a big weird thing bringing other weird things with it ever good?" said Decca.

"I don't.... when has there been a big weird thing around to bring other weird things before now?"

"Do you want to give it the benefit of the doubt?"

"The only movies where the aliens come and they aren't actually evil invaders are ones where they look like Jeff Bridges or Keanu Reeves," said Ian. "They're also boring as hell and I really want to see this thing more than I did fucking *Starman*."

"Good point," said Decca, "and I'm not usually the sort to advocate in favor of pop culture's portrayal of Others."

"What about the Iron Giant?" said Myra.

"Voiced by Vin Diesel. Handsome by proxy," said Ian.

"I think we're starting to lose track of things," I said. "What are we going to actually do, here?"

Everybody took that as an opportunity to sip their coffees.

After some time, Myra said: "I need to make a.... a cure, a solution to this thing. I think I accidentally brought it here with my work."

"Don't blame yourself," said Decca. "Yours wasn't the only art involved in this." She pointed towards Ian rather non-discretely.

"I have reasons to think that."

"I think," said Ian, "that I'm going to order the Greens, Eggs, and Ham. Then you guys are going to show me this—" he made air quotes with his fingers, "—alien."

7

After our business lunch, Myra decided to go back to her apartment and begin working on her potential solution. She was as forthcoming with details as Tzmir was in describing his method of arrival, which I suppose was appropriate. We bid her farewell and agreed to meet up later. Decca and I escorted Ian, briefed of the situation as best as we were able to understand it, to the gallery. He seemed—I'd say unusually accepting of what we had to tell him, but I'm not sure of what *usual* behavior should be when presented with anecdotal evidence of alien creatures trying to invade and/or obtain gallery representation in your hometown. Three displeased-but-accepting reactions to one mindless-cackling-wreck made Myra a bit of an outlier.

The gallery door was still intact and on its hinges when we arrived. I hesitated before unlocking it.

"Now you're sure you aren't going to go all Jamie Lee Curtis and cower in the corner when you see this thing?" I said.

Ian stuck his hands in his pockets and took a breath. "I don't think so? I mean, I can't say for sure until I'm actually in there, but it doesn't sound like anything worse than a John Carpenter flick. That includes *Prince of Darkness*."

"Alright. As long as you're encountering existential dread entirely of your own volition."

Decca peered up and down the street. "Coast's clear."

I unlocked the door, we slipped inside, and I locked it again behind us.

Tzmir was still there; halfway out of the same part of the wall, ultrapurple thing still happening where he intersected with it. He was fiddling with the fallen scaffolding pieces as we entered, idly reconnecting them at odd angles. I took a step towards it, then was overtaken by Ian who was practically sprinting over to the edge of the scaffolds.

"Can you shut it off? This thing is freakin' awesome!"

Tzmir stopped amusing itself and folded its claws across its chest, planting its arms squarely on the floor.

"My way will not be shuttered by the likes of you, without even so much as going through the proper binding rituals."

Ian gingerly stepped over one of his scaffolds to approach one of Tzmir's arms and poked it with a finger, then pressed his hand against it.

"I beg your pardon," Tzmir said.

"What did you use for this rig, vinyl tubes filled with mattress pads? Some baritone Smithie sitting back there with a megaphone?" He shuffled to the side to try and peer around Tzmir. "I figured they wouldn't even have an engineering program, what with being a girl school and all."

Decca looked understandably annoyed at that, but remained silent.

"The contents of my shell are none of your concern. Gregwithers, what is the purpose of bringing this one here?"

"Tzmir," I said, "this is Ian Irvin, another member of our... um, another gallery person."

"You've managed to herald my arrival to a very small populace."

"Small at the moment, but trust me, if you're going to get heralded then this is the guy you want to herald at."

"Total method acting, all the way," Ian said, looking back at me then up at Tzmir. He put a hand out to lean on Tzmir's forearm, which was about as tall as he was. "Can we break character and talk shop for a little bit?"

"Do you not understand the concept of personal space?" Tzmir raised its arm and made a sweeping motion with its fingers at Ian, who backed away from it.

"Can I talk to her? Will she hear me in there?" Ian said.

"Sure."

"It's not a Smith chick, Goofus," said Decca.

Ian cupped his hands around his mouth and shouted, "HI!"

Tzmir's headkelp quivered. "I possess adequate physical faculties to hear you, Ianirvin."

"Okay then. Sooo, hey! I'm the director here," Ian pointed towards himself with his thumbs. "You might be familiar with my zeitgeist-capturing film *The Fire That Refines Him*?"

"I would not be."

"Ah." Ian nodded, then turned to Decca and myself. "Does she have to stay in the zone like this? We're gonna need some more script revisions to work this thing in, and it would help to—"

"Ian, this isn't a clever animatronic thing from Smith, capable though our engineering department may be," said Decca.

"It's like we told you. Just look at what it's doing with its head and consider if that's something buildable," I said.

Ian turned around and observed Tzmir for a moment, who seemed to shrug slightly. Ian brushed his hand, which had touched Tzmir off on the side of his pants then turned back to us. It was difficult to tell in the dim purple-infused light of the gallery, but he seemed rather paler. There was a nervous smile on his face.

"Emergency meeting somewhere kinda private?"

"Excuse us a moment," I said to Tzmir, and we hurried over to my office.

Once inside, Ian took a deep breath and was about to speak when Decca pointed towards the door and said, "Oh no, nuh-uh, no." A couple of Tzmir's tentacles were hovering pensively by the doorframe. They shrank away with a mumbled apology from Tzmir and I shut the door. Then, with a raised finger, Decca said, "Don't tell me you're not going to help just because it isn't a fan of yours, because oh have I got n—"

"No, it's not about that. If that thing is actually the thing that it is then it looks straight-up fucking evil."

Decca's face brightened. "I know, right? So you're in?"

"I mean I don't want to be alone in a room with that thing. It shouldn't fucking *be.* How's it even fucking hearing us?"

"The same way that it's poking out halfway through the wall without some giant crayfish-bottom poking through into the hemp clothing store on the other side."

"Which is...?"

"Squid magic?" said Decca. "It said that it folds things."

"Maybe it *is* in the clothing store," I said.

"Well whatever the hell it's doing, it creeps me the fuck out."

"Look, Ian," I said. "We don't disagree about how evil this thing probably is. Myra thinks she has an idea to get rid of it, which is more than any of us have, but she needs time to do whatever it is she's doing. So, this thing has to be kept in the gallery away from prying eyes until then. Who knows what kind of coals we're going to get raked over if people find out that we're an accessory to some terror from beyond the stars?"

"If there isn't a law against it, they'll invent one," said Decca.

"If you want this thing as gone as we do, then we need to stop people from knowing it's here, until it isn't anymore. As far as anybody else knows, you're still using this place to film some cinematic tour-de-force. So we need you to maintain that facade."

Ian took a deep breath, ran his hands through his hair, and exhaled a drawn-out *"fuuuuuuck."*

"You're sure that thing isn't going to just eat me while I'm trying to pretend like I'm filming a movie here. If you're just trying to get back at me for playing fast and loose with the grant...."

I suppose, in hindsight, there was some schadenfreude in seeing Ian so distraught, but I was somewhat more concerned with saving my friends' and my own collective hide at the moment.

"That's all way too minor to care about in light of recent tentacley events," I said. "And I don't think it's particularly interested in eating people."

"It isn't in a position where it needs to be evasive about what it wants," said Decca.

Ian paced in a small circuit with his chin held in his hand. It seemed kind of exaggerated, but did produce results.

"Do you know if my guys got to bring in any of the cameras?"

I thought back to the various things I'd seen people not really assembling the previous day. "I'm not sure."

"Do you have a problem with me keeping any footage I happen to get of this thing in the process of distracting it?"

"Not at all."

"Ideally," Decca said, "it's going to be dead or banished or something when we're done, so you aren't going to be able to do any re-shoots."

Ian smirked. "Most of my first flick was done in one take, and if I can get that remarkable caliber of performance—" Decca rolled her eyes at that but Ian seemed not to notice, "—out of college students, I think I can handle a slime-crab-bastard-thing like that. Hell, it talks like dudes I know." He approached the door, opened it slightly and stuck his head out. After he brought it back in, he said: "Looks like there might be a camera case out there. I can play Seasick B. Demille out there for a while, but you've got to promise me you aren't going to take long because fuck that thing."

"I don't know how long Myra's going to take on whatever she's doing, but we'll keep you updated. We're headed over to her place as soon as we leave here."

"Okay. All in." Ian held a hand out, palm down, towards Decca and myself. I placed my hand over his, and Decca regarded us with bemusement for a moment.

"C'mon, Epitaph, we're all in on this," said Ian.

"Whatever blows your hair back, brah" she said, then added her hand on top.

"Alright, we're doing this! Gamefaces," said Ian. He then turned, threw open the door, and walked out with his head held high. We followed as he strode right up to the perimeter of scaffolding before Tzmir.

"Okay, biggie, what's your name?"

"Tzmirtalhuanchnivaalnimrtchuul."

Ian sucked on his teeth. "Yeaaah, that isn't gonna fly with the overseas market. Can I call you Cthulhu or something?"

Tzmir thumped a fist down on the floor, apparently as lightly as a fist that size can thump.

"You'd do well not to confuse the two of us in polite

company, unless you want to get branded as a cephalocist."

Ian looked at me, and I passed the look on to Decca, who shrugged and muttered: "Just go with it."

"Alright, my bad; how about we go with an honorific, like The Beast of the Painting, or The Horror from—Where You're From?"

"Well, I'm technically from the same place as you, if you only map spatial locations using three axes."

Ian adopted a thinking pose again.

"The Horror from Here isn't going to put butts in seats, it sounds like an expose on child poverty. But we'll work on that, we'll focus group something." Ian clapped his hands together then spread his arms wide. "Tzmir, baby, we're going to herald your arrival with a full-on media blitz, and this is gonna take some prep. People are going to want to know all about you and your artistic vision, and any other senses you possess that human minds can't comprehend. I don't know how you, er, guys are used to doing things like press junkets—"

"Traditionally we make our presence known to select neurotic individuals who then create maniacally-written records of their encounters, which are then gathered for cataloging in the Great Library of Pnakotus."

"That might be all well and good if you want to be a piddly little outsider artist, but you don't want to roll the dice and hope they come up Henry Darger." Ian accompanied that with a pantomimed dice-rolling motion. "I get the feeling that you think a little bigger than that."

"Trust me, your language lacks proper terminology for the dimensions encompassed by my thought processes."

"All the more reason that you're gonna need the human touch to help build your brand."

Decca and I left Ian blowing industry-speak smoke at Tzmir, and I hadn't realized until then how much the normal timbre of his voice seemed like a used car salesman's. If Tzmir's body language was comparable to humans, for what parts of his body were recognizable, he seemed to be taken in by Ian's shtick, so we figured it was safe to excuse ourselves for a little while.

We picked up some of the excess pizzas from my place and drove to Myra's building; with Decca lamenting "the loss of productive capacity to the whims of bourgeois affect" as we pulled up, though once inside she did agree that the elevator was really cool.

"So what are the odds she relapsed and we find her boarded up in her own bedroom gibbering about demons in the wallpaper?" she asked as we began our ascent.

"I really hope not—she's always seemed like an excessively stable person outside of that incident. But, I guess there's really no way to account for what kind of effect the emergence of a giant lobster-chested squid-person from a magic purple dimension will have on someone."

"Stable by artist standards? She did have both of her ears."

"Stable by most people's standards."

"So, is sheee—"

I knew how that question was going to end, recalling the previous day's conversation with Myra.

"No, she doesn't have a regular day job. She dove straight in to commercial-type art right after graduation, zero time in the service industry afterwards."

Decca sighed and pinched the bridge of her nose.

The elevator stopped, and I led us to Myra's apartment door. I knocked with my free hand, Decca held both of hers up with fingers crossed.

"Not gibbering, not gibbering, not gibbering..."

The bolt slid and the door opened on Myra, who was looking quite sane—if you didn't factor in the odd bits of plaster and decoupage she was adorned with, or the Panic at the Disco t-shirt she was wearing.

"Hey guys," she said, then noticed the pizzas. "Please tell me one of those is pineapple."

"I knew it, she's gone total Arkham on us," said Decca.

Myra cracked a smile at that and picked a fleck of gluey newspaper from her bangs.

"Go ahead and straight-edge your way out of tasty things, more for Greg and me."

Myra took the pizza boxes and ushered us in to her apartment, which was in its usual *in mixedmedia res* state, and told us to make ourselves at home. She detoured briefly to the kitchen with the pizzas, while Decca and I observed the living room slash studio space. There were two plaster hand-shapes on a couch that had been pushed out of the way to make space for a large paper-and-plaster-and-framework thing that was either drying or molting, depending on what Myra was planning on doing with it. Decca probably didn't know that thing was out of the ordinary, and took in the rest of the room with that exaggerated curiosity most people adopt when invited in to someone else's home for the first time.

"If I didn't know you were a working artist, that would've been my first guess upon seeing this place," she said.

"Well, I try not to give false impressions," said Myra. "Why are these pizzas cold?"

"They were unwittingly purchased yesterday afternoon."

"What are you building in here?" I said.

"Ah shmahmahm," said Myra through a mouthful of pizza as she walked in to the room.

Decca turned her attention to the shapeless thing. "A shaman?"

"Sorry," said Myra after swallowing, "I said 'a

statement.'"

"Nothing good has come of that word in the art world so far. Just look at the Manifestians going around reading theirs aloud and sending people's statues ballistic through others' work," I said.

"You want to kill the monster with inspirational art," said Decca.

Myra swallowed another bite of her pizza with a frown. "I don't give a hoot if it inspires anybody, it's more of a sort of personal atonement." She tucked the remaining crust behind an ear, brushed her hands on the sides of her pants and sat cross-legged at a coffee table where she'd arranged some paint tubes. She began unscrewing caps and blobbing them on to a palette. "The last real art-for-arts-sake thing I did was back in college. I was involved with this collective who'd formed out at Miskatonic U, but were miffed that the school didn't have any sports teams and transferred over. We attempted a couple weird consciousness-expanding art-phenomenon things that fizzled out. Turned out they were a bunch of goon-y losers, and I kind of wrote serious art off due to the negative association." She looked about her and, for lack of a brush, began blending some blobs of paint with her fingers. "I sold out, and the universe decided to sic a giant cephalopod on me. I need to make karmic amends for this."

"Well, in selling out's defense, the lobby of Baystate Medical Center has never looked so non-representational," said Decca.

"Quip all you want, anything corporate will pay top dollar for things that go over their heads." Myra hefted her palette, stood, and regarded the statue for a moment. "What kind of vehicle did you guys come in?"

"A car," I said. The look I received from Myra told me I wasn't as helpful as I'd expected.

"I... don't actually know what make the thing is," said

Decca.

"There's a tape measure in one of the kitchen drawers, could you get me the interior dimensions of whatever you've been putting your Free Peltier bumper stickers on? We need to make sure we can transport this thing when it's finished."

I went in to the kitchen and got the tape measure out of her silverware drawer, as Decca took it upon herself to explain the severity of Mr. Peltier's situation. At what sounded like a natural break in her monologue, I came back in to the living room, and we went down to her car as Myra kept working at her statue.

My phone rang while we were on our way out to the parking lot, and I showed the screen to Decca. It was Ian. I answered.

"Hey, Greg, on a scale of one to ten, how many guys would you let me bring on to help this look like an actual set?"

"Pardon?"

"What does he want?" said Decca.

I covered the mouthpiece. "He wants some guys."

"We need to have it look like something's actually going on here. I mean, if people just keep walking by and seeing lights and hear that damn tooting noise that Tzmir keeps doing, they're going to get suspicious. And you know there's a store on the same block called The Hempest; these people don't need help with being paranoid. If we make it look like a shoot in progress, then everything has an explanation."

I thought about it briefly. It seemed like a sensible request, and I didn't really see how he could go and twist having a couple other people around to his advantage.

"I guess you could invite a few people you know you can trust. But make sure they can keep the world's biggest, slobbering secret."

"If it's at all possible, I'll have them thinking this thing is just foam rubber and a method actor."

"Make sure you keep an eye on them for any gibbering, and remove them from the scene immediately if they start. MassHealth might not cover alien-induced fits of insanity."

"Sure thing. I got this in the bag. Talk to you later."

Then he hung up.

"Ian is probably going to bring a few more people into the inner circle."

"Whatever the hell for?" Decca shouted, leaning halfway into the backseat of her car. There was a hollow clunking noise and she stumbled forward, then walked herself back upright with her hands. "My back seats fold down! Who'd'a frickin' thought?" She *slinked* the tape measure shut for emphasis. "Whatever she's working on should fit in here with that little revelation. Let's just hope we don't have to transport Tzmir's giant corpse after it does whatever she expects it to."

We returned to Myra's studio with the news. She'd located a brush and was busy daubing paint on different portions of whatever the statue was supposed to be. Decca walked partly around the statue and extended the tape measure across its widest point.

"My car's got room enough for your centerpiece, *and* it has a sticker informing you how you can pay for the ride," she announced.

"Um, that's good," said Myra.

Decca *slinked* the tape measure again and walked into the kitchen. I brushed most of a dried handprint off the couch and took a seat. Myra continued daubing. Her statue at this point looked like it had started as a nearly-human-sized stick figure made of wooden dowels jammed into clay at the joints, kneeling with its arms upraised. It then had a head and uneven musculature added with plaster and papier-mâché. Myra was adding bright orange and deep red paint at points in what didn't seem to be any particular pattern.

"So, do you mind people observing your creative

process?" I said.

She paused and placed the end of her brush against her bottom lip in thought, cursed after a second when she realized it was the paint end, then wiped her mouth on a shoulder.

"I don't normally, because most of my stuff is just abstract-by-rote. Pick a medium I have enough of handy, put on some music and do what other art I've seen has done until I get tired of oblique angles, maybe attach a spinny bit if it's going to be outdoors, then voila." She made a little flourish in the air with her paintbrush at that. "That's what I think pissed the universe off, though, so I'm trying to go about this the legit artist way. I'm just letting the muse take hold and trying to express something actual. From in here," she tapped the brush, paint end again, against her t-shirt. "Oh dammit."

"S'just pop punk, nothing of value was damaged," said Decca, taking a seat on the couch with a plate of pizza.

Myra smirked and resumed intentional painting.

After a moment of observation, Decca asked: "So what are you actually expressing with this thing?"

Myra angled her nose upwards. "A lady never asks, and a lady never tells."

"Don't go all *Death of the Author* on me, I've been embedded in darkest academia for long enough to see through that get-out-of-accountability-free card."

Myra turned, cleared her throat, and gestured towards me with the paintbrush.

"Greg's a middleman by trade, he gets a pass on it," said Decca. "You should have some kernel of an idea of what would drive someone to make this thing what it is."

Myra jabbed two eyespots on what I guess was supposed to be the face-part of her statue.

"Joie de vivre? Some unquantified sense of the richness of life which I've failed to adequately express through all my other work due to its commercial bent, and its lack has been personified in the form of that damned thing that's writing a press release in the gallery before it does whatever the hell it's actually going to do. Probably try to eat us." She set her palette down and looked at the statue for a moment with her head tilted quizzically. Then she picked the palette back up, poked the statue's unhardened head with a free hand, then jammed the palette halfway in to the material so that it stuck out diagonally across what looked like it was the statue's face. Seeming content with her new addition, she exchanged her brush with her old pizza crust and dropped herself onto a matching chair next to the couch, leaning against one armrest with her legs draped over the other. "I've no idea where else to go with this thing, but I'm not done. You guys can turn on the TV if you want, I need to recharge a bit."

Myra continued intermittently dabbling with her statue as Decca and I watched some British sitcom that made me weirdly uncomfortable, which I'd thought would be difficult considering the day I'd had prior to that. Then I got a text from Ian:

- *Handling this LIKE. A. BOSS. Can't explain on the phone without you letting Decca swear at me. Just watch the news at 7.*

"Guys, I think there's been a development."

"What do you mean?" said Myra.

"At the gallery."

"Oh what the fuck now?" said Decca, proving that Ian was more perceptive than we gave him credit for.

I took the slightly paint-y remote from the coffee table and switched the TV to W-MAS. At that moment, Sy Becker was giving his typical overly enthusiastic endorsement of some movie or another.

"Why are we switching from an actual show to shitty

adver-tainment for whatever-the-heck," Decca asked as she reached for the remote. "Give it here. Mine." I held my arm out to the side and leaned away from her. Fortunately, the program transitioned back to the anchor at the news desk before Decca could deploy any strategic poking.

"And, it looks like Hollywood isn't the only place getting in on the action," said the anchor. "Unannounced shooting for a film began on the streets of Treebridge earlier today, an event that took some residents by surprise."

Decca froze with a finger aimed precariously towards my ribs.

It cut to blurry phone-camera footage of a sort of human-shaped thing, squat and greenish with a blunt face, loping along the sidewalk outside of an Indian restaurant downtown.

The thing on the footage turned the corner on to the street the gallery was on, then it cut to another reporter talking to the teenage kids who had recorded it. They were imitating the thing's walk, and describing it as "a big scaly fishguy." One cupped their hands over their mouth and moved them up and down, fingers splayed, to describe its teeth.

"Oh, I'm gonna garrote that bastard," said Decca. Myra sat in her chair, wide-eyed but otherwise expressionless.

It then cut back to the anchor in the studio. "After receiving several calls about the incident, police arrived on the scene and questioned local filmmaker Ian Irvin, who admitted to being behind the stunt and offered residents an apology."

It cut to footage of Ian, standing outside the gallery with the previous field reporter holding a microphone out to him.

"Yeah, I'd put in for all the necessary permits on Friday," he said, brandishing a very familiar handful of papers for effect, "but I guess they're still busy stamping the things in triplicate. You'd think that someone trying to get a new local industry off the ground would've lit a fire under 'em, but hey, it's their economy, y'know?"

"New local industry?" said the reporter.

"Hollywood North! We're showing all the rest of the film world that this is where you gotta go to get things done. Have a guy in a fish costume run down the middle of the street, they don't care up here! Bunch of stoic New Englanders will just stay out of your way. We had hidden cameras in the storefronts and nobody even batted an eye! Right here, right now, I'm making my declaration: Treebridge's name is going to be on the map for more than just lesbians and leaf-watchers."

It cut back to the news anchor, who closed the segment with: "The mayor's office has declined to comment on the processing of Irvin's permits, though a representative has affirmed the office's dedicated support of local industry."

Decca pumped a fist into the air and bounced up from the couch. "People bought it! The smarmy bastard used his powers for good!"

"What in the hell was that thing?" said Myra.

"I'll find out," I said, and sent a text to Ian with that same question.

A moment later, my phone chirped with his response:

- *Won't try spelling its name in but it's like something everybody makes jokes about living in Boston Harbor. Pals with Tzmir. Smells how it looks like it would.*

"Apparently it's exactly what the kids thought it was."

"Is your statue finished?" said Decca.

"I guess I'm happy with it, yeah," said Myra. "We should probably get it over there."

"And then what happens? Will we use it to just, I dunno, *dispel* Tzmir and the fish guy?"

"I'm solving this like an artist," said Myra, chin held high, "I'll just see what inspiration strikes me when we arrive."

8

After some experimental hoists to figure out what parts of the statue probably wouldn't snap off in the process, we managed to get it in to the elevator, which had ample room for the three of us alongside it, slid the door shut and pressed the down button. In the interest of not just standing there breathing heavily, I asked Myra if the statue had a name.

She pursed her lips for a moment then said, between air quotes: "Narrative of Soul Against Soul."

Decca flat-out chortled at that.

"What?" said Myra.

"Nothing, that's just.... it's an appreciative laugh. I guess I pegged you as more of a synth-pop type is all."

After a spirited bout of rotating and no-it's-caught-on-something, interspersed with moments of standing around with our hands on our hips, we were able to fit it into Decca's trunk and back seat, with room enough for a third passenger to still wedge in.

"I hope we can find out how Tzmir does that whole space-folding thing he was talking about," said Decca when we'd finished. "It's probably one of those 'Things Man Was Not Meant To Know,' which means it should be fine for Myra and me to learn it, at least."

Before we got in to the car, Myra had an epiphany and had us wait while she ran back inside. She came out some minutes later carrying a battered, spiral-bound notebook. "Notes from my college days with the Misky U troupe," she said. "Something in here might help me figure out what it is we should be doing."

We took our seats, with Myra in back, draping a protective arm over her statue; we drove through the city towards the gallery. Once we got downtown, however, we found the street that the gallery was on had been blocked off for two blocks on either side by orange police barricades. There wasn't a game that night—it couldn't have been a run-of-the-mill "Red Sox lost" riot; nor an equally probable "Red Sox won" riot. We circled around the adjacent block and wound up parking in the public lot on its opposite side, which was free at night. The lot was downhill from the gallery, but after gingerly unloading Myra's statue through the trunk, we were able to carry it up to the front door with a minimal amount of stopping and cursing. We got some odd looks from people seated outside at the restaurants we passed, but honestly, we weren't anything weirder than the busker who'd sit at a local bus stop while painting pictures of entirely different bus stops.

Foot traffic seemed to be allowed on the street outside the gallery, though it was entirely barred to cars from both directions for the entire length of the block. The gallery itself had hand-written signs in the windows that read QUIET FILMING IN PROGRESS. I didn't know why Ian thought making a silent film would be an ideal cover story, but it seemed to be doing the job well enough. I knocked firmly on the gallery door.

"Read the sign!" came from within.

I took out my phone and texted *DOORBELL* to Ian, and seconds later the door was unlocked. I looked to Decca and Myra.

"How are we doing this?"

"Why don't you guys go in and see what the situation is with the fishman—"

Decca *ahem*ed.

"—okay, with the fishperson, and I'll wait out here with Narrative of Soul Against Soul, then if it seems like it's a safe time to do what we've got to do, come out and signal me."

"How are we going to know that?"

"I... you'll probably just get a sense for it. Go on."

Decca and I entered the gallery. The lights were on and Tzmir looked all the stranger for it—its limbs did seem rather flabby and rubbery under regular lighting conditions, though that effect might have been enhanced by the scaffolding having been reassembled next to it; and some lengths of rope leading to it being strung loosely around the wrists of its humanoid arms. It was leaning over Newsie's shoulder, or rather looming ominously above him, as he was showing it and the fishperson something in a magazine. Ian and Lumberjack were sitting on a bench they'd pulled against the wall next to my office door, working on a laptop. It looked like they had discovered a couple of cameras among the cases the crew left, and they were set up facing Tzmir, though they didn't appear to be on or plugged in to anything. The gallery did smell faintly like one would imagine an enclosed space inhabited by alien sea monsters would.

Ian waved at us as we approached. "This is getting even more insane, ain't it?"

"Gregwithers and Deccalyne," bellowed Tzmir. "News of my arrival shall now be even more dramatic when revealed to the populace! We are conducting a screen test!" It gestured, with its claws, towards the ropes around its arms.

"Yeah, would you mind filling us in on the details of our newest arrival there?" I gestured towards the fishperson. It seemed to be about 5'8" accounting for a slight hunch, and its head joined directly to its shoulders with little in the way of a neck. Its large eyes were solid black, like a shark's, and there was at least one row of jagged teeth visible in the thing's broad mouth.

"So that trumpet-y noise Tzmir had been making," said Ian, "was apparently to summon these things."

"You pluralized that," said Decca.

"Yeah, Tzmir says that it says that there will be others. I guess this guy was just the quickest of them."

I had to wonder how accurate a statement that could have been when, at that moment, it seemed to be quite interested in an issue of *Guitar Monthly*.

"The arrival of Dagon's children is imminent—soon Ianirvin tells me we shall begin a process known as principal casting," said Tzmir.

Ian gave an exaggerated nod. "Yep. Once we figure out which of... what's supposed to be this fish-looking, fish-smelling dude's name again?"

"Gaknaugak," said Lumberjack.

"Once the rest of Gak's people turn up. I don't know that they're all going to be as photogenic as Gak here. Oh, dude, let's show 'em the glow!"

Lumberjack went over to the wall where the light switches were and turned them off. After a moment, lit only by the faint purple glow happening behind Tzmir, a couple lines of teal bioluminescence shimmered across Gak's face, arms, and down its side. Decca and I both reflexively *oohed* at the sight, though once the lights went back on, I was quickly back to thinking Gak was some kind of abomination against God.

"Is it intelligent? Or at least not as aggressive as it looks?" said Decca.

"It's fine. I don't think it can speak English, but Bryan still has all his fingers after playing with it for like an hour."

Decca cautiously approached Newsie—Bryan, apparently —and Gaknaugak. I continued with questioning Ian.

"So what happened with the street outside?"

"They called my bluff, man! The city didn't want to look like they'd gone and misplaced some important paperwork, so they're totally bending over backwards to accommodate whatever I tell them I'd filed for. Got them to block off the road just for safety's sake, and I can probably get us both some hefty tax breaks out of the deal."

"Ian, what on Earth *did* you file for?" I said.

He spread his arms and grinned. "I didn't, that's the beauty of it! Everybody wants a piece of what Hollywood North's got going on, the city would cordon off Interstate Ninety-One if they thought it would get them some film moguls spending tourist money in town, not to mention the chance of celebrity sightings. I told you, I got this in the bag."

"Do they know this is supposed to be a low budget indie production?"

"Well, I'm certainly not going to tell them. Are you?"

I paused to consider and, honestly, realized that I wouldn't if I had the opportunity. It wouldn't have been believable if I did, considering that we had what as far as anybody else knew, were some elaborate and expensive-looking specimens of Smith engineering.

"Anything we need to do, we're covered as long as we drop the H-bomb in to our request."

"Hollywood North!" shouted Lumberjack, and fist-bumped Ian.

"We shall all proceed down the Hall of the Woods in due time, resplendent in our rugosity," said Tzmir. It continued on in that manner, seemingly content with expounding about itself to nobody in particular.

Gaknaugak turned towards our group and croaked something that sounded approximately like "Haaawaanaat."

Decca leveled a glare at Ian that could have made a record player skip.

"You're teaching this thing dudebro call-and-response bullshit?"

Ian turned away and slid down lower on the bench, feigning embarrassment and holding the laptop up over his face.

"It's sort of just been doing that on its own," said Bryan.

Decca rolled her eyes and returned to her own attempts to interact with Gaknaugak. She seemed to be gesturing towards a bracelet it had on one of its arms that I hadn't noticed before.

Ian gestured for me to come closer, and he leaned over to whisper: "How far along are you guys coming with the killing-this-thing plan? Because with Gackie in the mix we're actually working on some ideas to salvage this production."

Lumberjack nodded enthusiastically. "The Creature from the Connecticut River, man."

I tried to replicate Decca's earlier glare. "Don't you start defecting on us now. We've got what I guess is the weapon ready for deployment right outside," I whispered back. "Myra's just catching herself up on old school magic-with-a-K stuff while we're in here scouting out the area. Which seems pretty scouted to me."

"Right on!" Ian gave a thumbs up, holding an open hand between it and Tzmir to hide it. "So is there going to be, like, a blast radius or fallout or anything? Are we safe just sitting over here?"

"I'm kind of assuming Myra will tell us if we need to move or anything. I don't think we're close enough to get crushed if Tzmir just instantly keels over. Maybe get your other person away from him."

"Gotcha." Ian put two fingers in to his mouth and made a sort of rough exhaling sound. "You really need to show me how to do that sometime, dude," he said to Lumberjack, who put his fingers into his beard and whistled quite loudly. Decca, Bryan, and Gaknaugak paused to look at us, and Ian waved them over.

"Alright, clear the scene," he called out.

Bryan hurried over. Decca gently took hold of Gaknaugak's arm and led it over with her.

"What are you thinking?" she said.

"I believe it's time to get 'Operation Get Myra to End This Damned Thing' underway."

"Alright, brace both yourselves and Gaknaugak," Decca said, exiting the gallery.

"Ianirvin, the time has arisen when we shall photograph my principles!" Tzmir reached up and brushed its fingers through its headkelp. "Moral invectives may yet prove valuable to my widespread acceptance."

"Sure," Ian called back. He rose from his seat and handed the laptop to Lumberjack. "So, look, I don't know anything about you things' anatomy. Can we put makeup on you? Do we need to pat you down with wet towels like a beached whale or anything? We want to have you looking your greenest, after all."

"I'd be wholly unsuited for meta-terrestrial excursion were I not capable of producing my own protective coatings," Tzmir said. It appeared to tense up momentarily, then the fleshy parts of its body began to glisten faintly with some substance it sweat out.

Ian, the crew, and I all blanched at the sight of it but consummate charlatan that he was, Ian continued on.

"Awesome, you're a total budget saver!" He clasped his hands in front of him, spun on a heel, mouthed *Jesus Christ* to us, then spun back around and marched towards Tzmir.

"So, no pressure here—we might be able to do it in post if we really need to, but it would be great if we could get a big grand entrance shot of you coming through whatever it is you're doing back there. The purpley jazz."

Tzmir's chest heaved and it emitted what I suppose was a sigh for something its size, though it sounded more like an air conditioning unit warming up.

"Look, let's not let this information make it out to the general populace, for reputation's sake. Portal dimensions are traditionally set at the time of invocation and, well," it pressed the tips of its index fingers together, twisting them back and forth, "when the ritual to summon me was originally undergone, I was not so Elder a God as I am at present."

The door to the gallery opened, and Decca slid the doorstop in to place.

"Ah, I get you," Ian said. He was standing next to one of the assembled cameras, which he grabbed a hold of and began folding its tripod. "Y'know, since a camera adds ten pounds, why don't we make sure there's only one of them on you at any given time?"

"It would be appreciated, yes." Tzmir clenched a fist before itself. "The Children of Dagon will surely aid in the unfolding of my full bodily glory to this plane upon their arrival, but for the present time my ovipositors must remain beyond the veil."

"Ovipositor? But you hardly know 'er!" Decca shouted from the doorway, holding one end of the statue, with Myra on the other end. They crab-walked it towards Tzmir as Ian scrambled back to our bench, carrying his camera.

"I'm trying to save the world, and you're backing me up with dad jokes," said Myra.

"Just trying to relieve a little tension," said Decca.

The two of them deposited the statue several feet in front of Tzmir, then Decca scurried over to join our group by the bench. She, myself, Ian, and Lumberjack crouched down behind the bench. Bryan, without room, stood a little ways behind us with Gaknaugak.

"Ianirvin, it would appear that Deccalyne and the crying one have intruded in the frame," said Tzmir. "You'd assured me that the wards you'd placed at the entrance would be sufficient."

Ian paused in the process of angling the bench between us and Tzmir. "Oh, this is some... this must be some kind of warlock sorcery!" he said, looking surprised.

Myra took her bent-in-half notebook out of her back pocket, flexed it straight, then opened it. Tzmir's headkelp drew in close, like time-lapse footage of a flower closing its petals.

"I'm not familiar with the glyphs you've engraved upon that book of yours."

"That's just a Tsunami Bomb sticker on the cover," Myra said, "but that's not the important part. How do you feel about *this*?" Myra turned the book around and held it spread open with both hands, to face Tzmir. We were a ways off to the side, so I couldn't see what it might have contained.

"Your book's contents are as ephemeral to me as the emblem upon its cover. What exactly are you attempting to do here, impress me? With line art encompassing a mere two dimensions?"

"Okay, words now," Myra said. She turned the notebook back to herself and began to read aloud a string of nonsensical syllables from it.

Tzmir leaned on one elbow and began drumming its fingers, which was actually a pretty intimidating gesture from something its size—the paintings on the wall rattled slightly while it did so. Then it seemed to realize the effect it was having and stopped.

"Is there much more to your presentation, crying one? I must admit that I'm not at all impressed by the... free-verse poetry, is it, that you're doing? And I don't believe I'm presently in need of an intern or personal assistant, though you may be able to inquire with Ianirvin. He's handling all of those matters for me while I'm preparing my current exhibition for its debut."

Myra shut her notebook and threw it to the floor with a *thwap*, then gestured to her statue with both hands.

"Really," she said, "nothing? I'm recanting my fucking commercial ways and having strayed from the path of earnest inspiration here!"

Tzmir leaned forward, and its headkelp fanned out in the direction of Myra's statue.

"I'm not familiar with your prior body of work, but you seem to have strayed on to a path of amateurish derivation and aesthetic hodge-podge. What of this will skew observers' perceptions, shining an inmost light at the audient void? I don't even know what sort of mixed message you were trying to send with that palette through the golem's forehead.

"And that's to say nothing of your spoken word performance which, despite your passable incorporation of Eldrish vocabulary, made neither cogent points nor memorable impressions. Suffice to say, I find your work to lack appreciable depth, breadth, and scope."

"This is supposed to banish you," Myra said, with a quaver in her voice.

"Good. I'd thought it was supposed to *impress* me," said Tzmir. It then placed a large hand palm-down in front of the statue and curled one finger beneath it, against the floor. Those of us behind the bench all ducked at the same time when we recognized what was about to happen. There was an enormous cracking sound, followed by numerous things skittering on the floor and a plaster lump with a paint palette embedded in it flying over the bench, landing some feet behind us and cracking open.

I want to say it didn't make sense that Myra's plan

hadn't worked, but I don't know what a sensible plan to deal with such an event would have looked like. Ian and Decca had gone pale and wide-eyed, and I assume I looked much the same.

"Come the hell on!" Myra shouted.

I peered back over the top of the bench. She was standing next to the collapsed legs of her statue, arms spread out. Tzmir seemed to have curled his headkelp in to a tight ball solely so it could rest its head in an open hand as an expression of boredom.

"Whatever direction you come to is of no concern to me as long as it's decidedly away from my future showings. I'm not particularly looking to engage in any sort of collaborations that might sully my own artistic vision by association." Tzmir then made a dismissive waving-away gesture towards Myra. "Fear not, Ianirvin, this woman is no warlock. Come forth and let us discuss the practical side of recreating my grand unfolding for the camera!"

"Just a minute," Ian shouted over the top of the bench. "We're discussing, um, not letting other fans approach you like that." He ducked back down and turned to Decca and myself with wide eyes, shaking his head frantically back and forth.

"You said this thing was going to get dead and I wouldn't have to pretend to not hate knowing it exists. I'm not going. That thing should be on fucking fire and falling off the side of a bridge. Onto some rocks."

Lumberjack made a flourish with his hand, which suddenly had a Zippo lighter in it. "We can try one of those right now."

I did my best to shout-whisper. "You're going to burn down my entire gallery and several peoples' collected work if you try smoking that monster out."

Decca reached over and put a hand on Ian's and my arms, them pointed to Gaknaugak, who was observing us with a wide-eyed expression. Though I think that's just how its face was shaped.

"Do you understand us?" Ian said to it.

It tilted its head to the side at an angle. The universal signal of incomprehension.

Lumberjack held his lighter out to it. Decca *what-the-helled* and lunged across Ian and I to pull his arm down.

"Dude, take that somewhere," Ian said.

Bryan took Gaknaugak by the arm and led it in to my office.

I heard Myra's footsteps approaching the bench, and she called out, "Which Finn's is open latest?" as she did so

"The one on Redfern Ave, I think," said Lumberjack.

"I'm going there. Show up or don't," she said. She made a wide circle around the bench and picked up her palette, which still had half of the statue's head attached to it. "Second time today I've had to fucking do this." She walked out of the gallery holding the head under one arm.

Decca jabbed an authoritative finger at Ian.

"You go out there and humor that squiddlything until we figure out how to kill it, or so help me Dark Gods..."

"What am I even distracting it until? Your magic artist friend who brought it here just failed to shoo it away."

"She's not supposed to be magic," I said, at a loss for any kind of explanation for what we thought we were doing.

"We can *all* see that now," Ian said.

"We frickin' missed something," said Decca.

There was a purposeful silence after that, as though everybody in our little cluster knew the others needed to concentrate on either thinking, worrying, or proper use of accelerants. Then, Decca *thonked* a fist onto the floor to break it.

"There was another piece of art involved in the accident," she said.

"The Verrick painting," I said, then added, "the angle-y line thing nobody else liked," when the first explanation fell flat.

"Exactly. Since we've ruled out Myra, that crazy dude is the only other party involved. He must have summoned a sea demon because you broke his painting! And you were worried he was just going to sue you."

"You just thought the wrong warlock had summoned the thing. Okay," said Ian.

"Oh ha ha, at least we have a plan B," said Decca. "Do you have his info somewhere, Greg?"

"Of course. Ian, go and play pretend with Tzmir, we have another idea."

"Nuh-uh, I still want it gone. I mean, I can work with the fishdude—it follows directions and it's got a face. Biggie's a full-on diva."

"Keep it busy for twenty four hours," said Decca, "and then you can set the thing on fire if we don't have a solution by then."

"Decca!" I shouted.

"Fuckin' A," said Lumberjack.

"I knew you were one of the guys," said Ian, with a joyful clap of his hands. "One more day of playing Jacques Cousteau then it's *Wicker Man* time. Let's do this."

Ian stood and hopped over the bench to get back to Tzmir as Decca and I went in to my office. Bryan was sitting in my chair, and Gaknaugak was standing by my desk, looking with what I assume curiosity looked like on its unusual facial features—at its reflection in my computer monitor.

"Can I, um, I was going to use that," I said.

Bryan shrugged. "I haven't been on this thing's bad side yet, and I don't think I want to try telling it that it can't do something."

I got his point. Fortunately, I still kept a Rolodex that Gak wasn't interested in, and I proceeded to dump it out onto my desk.

It was easy enough to find the card I was looking for amongst all the other colorful ones in the pile—it was grey print on a slightly different grey cardstock, not even laminated. All it said on the front was "Donald Verrick, Antinatalist," and a phone number with a 413 area code, so at the very least he probably wasn't located out in Boston or Arkham.

Gaknaugak picked up my computer monitor and turned with it, holding it at arm's length, still looking at its reflection. It touched its face with one hand. Replacing a computer monitor was probably the least of my troubles at that point, but still, I got Bryan to hand me the old bananas I'd left in my desk drawer from the previous morning. I dangled them out next to Gaknaugak to get his attention, and after looking at them for a moment he put the monitor down and took the bananas.

Out in the gallery, Ian seemed to be instructing Tzmir, who was sort of crouching down on its elbows against the wall.

"So you make like you just burst in and... what do you things do, do you have, like, a battle cry? That flute-thing you did to call Gackie doesn't really make for an intimidating presence."

"Ian, we're headed out. Keep your eyes peeled for the public," I called.

He turned, gave a thumbs up, then held out an arm and gestured to his wrist, which was still a convenient shorthand for time, even though nobody really wore watches anymore.

"Okay, you too," Decca said.

Then we left to go find a drunk and depressed woman carrying half of a plaster head.

I felt terrible for Myra, not just for her being somewhat-publicly insulted by Tzmir, but apparently for it totally misunderstanding her art. Which isn't to claim that I *do* understand her art, but at least I try not to draw such attention to it. I certainly remembered how I felt whenever I received my lackluster grades for most of the humanities electives I'd taken —they'd always sent me into a funk for a few days, even though I knew the timely delivery of a Witherpedic Pillowtop to the professor would bump it up to a passable "C."

Decca seemed even more concerned, and kept fidgeting with the lock in her ear as we walked. We didn't have much to say to each other on the way, we just knew we had to catch up with Myra before the Artistic Temperament did.

By the time we got to the right Finn's, Myra was already seated at a table in the back and had just started wringing a lime out above her drink. The statue head she'd brought with her was placed in the middle of the table as a glower-piece.

Decca placed a hand on my shoulder. "I bought last time," she said, then went over to Myra's table. I went to the bar, got a Guinness and a gimlet, and joined them. As I took a seat next to Decca, I noticed Myra's unusually festive glass.

"Did you really get a frozen margarita?"

"Something's got to lift my spirits! We're going to get eaten by a giant burbling monster because my art sucks, so I should be allowed to get girl-drink-drunk."

"Well we have good news," said Decca. "It might be some other guy who summoned Squidface, because Greg's chump friend's chump employees destroyed his painting."

"I wonder what *he's* drinking."

"It's a gimlet," I said.

"No, I meant... never mind. How is this good news?"

"Because I've got his contact info." I placed Verrick's card on the table in front of Myra. She squinted down at it. Admittedly, it wasn't the most convenient thing to read in subdued bar lighting.

"Okay. Want me to show what's left of my dumb statue

to him until he calls off the fish guys?"

"We're going to call him and ask him what the hell is going on and what we can do to get him to stop," said Decca.

"I'm willing to settle. Out of court. Whatever he wants," I said.

"There are other means of getting him to comply." Decca flicked her arm behind her, then out, and her baton extended with a smooth metal-sliding noise. Several other bar customers' heads turned.

Myra laughed, nearly choking on a *glug* of margarita as she did so. "Put that fucking thing away in here!"

Decca shrugged and re-collapsed it against the tabletop. "I'm just saying we have options here."

I slid Verrick's card back to me across the table and took out my phone. "So, how do we approach this? We can't get aggressive right out of the gate."

Everybody else took that as an opportunity to drink. I followed suit.

"Apologetic, maybe," said Myra. She fidgeted with the tiny umbrella in her glass.

"Try feigning total ignorance," said Decca.

"That much I can do."

"Just say you're calling to inform him that his painting has been damaged and you want to figure out how to proceed from there. See what information he's forthcoming with."

"You two want to advise me on this? Conference call?"

"We don't want him to hear this place's—" Decca tilted an ear upwards momentarily "—Godsmack, of damn course, while we're trying to talk business. Let's go outside."

"But... but drinking." Myra cupped her arms around her margarita glass.

"Alright, alright, I'll just call and turn to you guys if I'm in over my head."

I finished my gimlet, angled the card against the light so

I could make out Verrick's number, and dialed.

It rang. It rang twice. Then a third time. Then it picked up.

"May I ask who is calling," said a deep and cigarettey voice.

"Uh, is this Mr. Donald Verrick?"

"I was not inquiring as to my own name but yes, I am him."

I gave Decca and Myra a thumbs up.

"This is Greg Withers, of the Withers Local Art Gallery in Treebridge."

"I've seen the news."

I mouthed "he saw the news" to the others.

"So, um, I can assume that you're upset about the accidental—entirely accidental I assure you—damage to your painting."

"An accident." There distinctly was not a question mark there, though there was a small, snide laugh.

"Yes, it was completely an accident. So please call off your weird alien sea-men."

Decca winced.

"They're not mine."

I mouthed "they're not his" to the table.

Myra pulled a pen out of a pocket, scribbled on the palm of her hand and showed it to me. It said *what?* And below that, *why aren't we just talking?*

"You don't know what it is that you're involved in, do you," asked Verrick.

"I know there's a giant squid-thing prattling off a manifesto in the middle of my art gallery."

"The underlying realities of New England escape you."

"Look, I'm totally willing to settle this out of court for the value of your painting if it—"

There was another small laugh.

"This isn't about the painting. Or, rather, it's not about any particular emotional or financial investment of mine in the painting."

"That's good," I said.

The ensuing silence indicated to me that my answer was somewhat of a departure from what he was expecting.

"So, um, what is it about, then?"

"Come to my house tomorrow. I will enlighten you as to the particulars of your degenerate little town."

"Alright. We'll be there. Thank you," I said, then hung up and addressed the group. "He says that if we go see him tomorrow he'll apparently tell us what the deal is with Tzmir and them."

Decca raised her glass in response.

"So this has turned from a drink of remorse in to one of pensive celebration!"

Myra and I raised our glasses. Then I picked my phone back up and re-dialed Verrick's number. He answered, again, after the third ring.

"I presume," he said, "you are calling back because you have realized that my home address is not on my business card."

9

I was right in my assumption that Verrick lived on the 413 side of the state, though he did live in Ripton, which was a good way further up along Massachusetts' northern border. It would be a bit of a jaunt up the Mass Pike, but it was feasible to get there and back within the day if we lucked out and there wasn't any seasonal roadwork along the way.

After we'd finished our victory drinks at Finn's, it was decided that we would crash at my apartment, since I had sufficient couch space for three and the remaining leftover pizzas.

I was awoken that morning by repeated text message chirps from my phone. After rubbing the sleep out of my eyes, I saw they were from Ian.

-FUCK
-DUDE
-THERES MORE FUCK

I called Ian, since text did not seem to be the most efficient method for this discussion, and was greeted with some words in a similar cadence.

"What do you mean there's more," I asked, during a break in the profanity. "More Gaknaugaks?"

"I got here this morning and there were, like, seven more of them. They must have been traveling at night like Gackie did."

"Oh God, how did they get in? Did they break the front window?"

"Nah, that's all still intact. Maybe has some weird looking handprints on it or something, I didn't look too close. But the door is kind of scratched up around the handle and lock, so I guess Gackie figured out how to let them in."

"What are they actually doing in there?"

"They're hopping around and talking with Tzmir in a language that sounds like Gackie's name. Some of them have bags with them, one is holding a thick book-looking thing."

"What were they bringing in the bags?"

"I don't know, man, I haven't been able to talk at Tzmir since getting here. They look like they're orchestrating something. And I don't speak them-speak. Hold up—" there was some rustling from the other end of the line, "—oh dude they're setting out big dribbly candles, they're going full-on Wiccan up in here."

"Stop them! Do you think you—"

"Some husky chicks wearing JNCOs and combing their bangs over their faces are gonna show up if they keep on like this."

Of all the things I'd heard that week that I knew would get him slapped if I repeated them...

"God, man, fucking stop. Can you schmooze up and prevent them from doing whatever it is they're planning to do until we can figure out what we should do about what they're doing?"

"I can try but, well, you've seen those things' teeth. I don't want to get on their bad side. The one thing was fine because we could probably take it on if it came down to it, but now there's a fucking school of them. We're gonna need a bigger boat."

"I'm going to come by on our way out of town, I need to see this so we can tell our guy about it and we'll work on something to delay them—but seriously, stop the hell out of them for like fifteen minutes."

"I'll do what I can, but I'm not gonna get feeding frenzied over this. Oh! What do fish eat other than cans of brown flaky stuff?"

I actually didn't know the answer to that, but also wasn't at the point in the day where I had patience, so I just said, "cool," and hung up. I got dressed and went into the living room to inform the rest of the road-trip group of our slight detour. It always feels like a rude imposition waking somebody else up, but fortunately, Decca and Myra were already sitting at attention on their respective couches and chatting when I came in.

With the two of them waiting in the car so we technically weren't parked and didn't need to put quarters in the meter, I approached the gallery door carrying the remaining three-day old pizzas to help placate the new visitors. I knocked on the door with my free hand and, after a moment, Lumberjack peered around the edge of the curtain and unlocked it. I entered the gallery, he took the pizza boxes from me, and I surveyed the situation.

There were seven more Children of Dagon in the gallery. Six, including Gaknaugak, were just sort of standing around gazing vacantly at me, though I think that might have just been the shape of their eyes. Some of them sniffed at the air, then began to cautiously approach the new pizza-bearer.

Two others, who appeared to be wearing more of that silver jewelry I'd seen on Gaknaugak, were sitting on their haunches in front of Tzmir appearing to confer with each other. Tzmir seemed... lost in thought, I suppose; its headkelp were closed up like a flower bud. Ian was standing near the two Dagons, filming them with one of his cameras set up on a tripod. He looked up and waved me over to him, while he held a finger over his mouth. I walked over, trying not to let my shoes click on the hardwood floor. As I approached, I noticed that what I thought to be jewelry was actually a pair of headphones one of the Dagons was wearing, which were plugged in to Ian's laptop on the floor in front of them. Another wire extended from the laptop up in to Tzmir's headkelp.

"You wanted some time bought?" Ian whispered.

"What on Earth are you doing?"

"Shooting some B-roll, for one. For two," he cupped a hand over his mouth and called up to Tzmir, "are you digging it, biggie?"

Tzmir shook itself from its withdrawn state and lowered the headphones it was clutching inside its head with a single tentacle, placing them delicately on the floor next to the laptop.

"Your people have truly harnessed the fundamental forces of the universe to astounding ends."

"Thanks," I said to Tzmir, followed by a low, "what did you do to it?" to Ian. He was just looking at me with a self-satisfied grin. More self-satisfied than his usual grin.

"Gregwithers, I need to inform you of an additional project I plan to undertake. I will be composing a response to each of these sixty-nine love songs you've derived from the planet's magnetic field."

It took me a couple blinks' worth of time to process what had happened. I squinted at the laptop screen and saw that "Nothing Matters When We're Dancing" was playing. The Dagon with the headphones was faintly swaying side to side.

"It's, ah, it's about time somebody did! That's great! How are things going with your other project? I see you've got more of your people gathered here."

"The urban amelioration is underway—behold!" Tzmir croaked something and gestured towards one of the Dagons, who hefted a large cloth sack and waddled over to us with it. It then croaked an approximation of 'behold' and overturned the sack, sending what must have been a hundred some-odd brightly-colored hollow plastic balls *plokk*ing out on to the gallery floor.

"Witness the apotheosis of my aesthetic," said Tzmir.

I witnessed the plastic balls expanding like a slow puddle and could easily imagine one of the Dagons—or even Lumberjack—stepping on one and sliding Hanna Barbera style across the gallery, knocking paintings down as they flailed.

"You do seem to be a few thousand short of being able to fill an abandoned house with them," I said.

"This is mere proof of concept. Their material properties are pleasant and suitable to my needs." Tzmir clasped its humanoid hands together before it, picked up a plastic ball with one of its claws and *plokked* it against the floor. "All that remains is for you to provide Klutraklu with a money, so as to procure further supplies."

Ian had taken his camera over to the sack-carrier, Klutraklu I suppose, and made a sweeping gesture at the mass of balls. "Piiiick uuuup," he said, to a blank gaze from the Dagon, "agaaaaain for fiiiiilm. Caaameraaa." I didn't think the Dagons technically had pupils or irises, but a sliver of white appeared at the bottom of Klutraklu's eyes, as though it had rolled them.

I figured that asking where the original supply of balls had come from was irrelevant, or would probably be better explained by a nearby town's police blotter. Even if Ian and Lumberjack were following it with a camera and one of those big reflective umbrella-lamps, I didn't want one of those things leaving the gallery again. Nor did I feel like taking the time to correct Tzmir's idea of how money works.

"You know, I'm actually taking a little day trip out to Ripton, I'm sure there's got to be a couple Toys R' Uses along the way. Why don't I just stop in and buy up all their stock for you on my way back? Keep your Dagons here so they can help you with... what all are you actually preparing to do?"

"My responses to the love songs shall occupy me until this evening, then presuming timely delivery of the novelty orbs, I shall lead the Children of Dagon in the ritual of emergence when the moon aligns, and in full terrible glory I shall scamper to Springfield and deliver my conceptual brilliance unto their degenerate little town!"

That was it, then. We had until some unspecific time that night to get Verrick to do whatever he had to get done to get rid of Tzmir, or else all of Tzmir would be here and I had no intention of seeing what the rest of it looked like, let alone allowing it to go around peeling the roofs off of dumpy Colonial-style houses and telling everybody I'd paid it to do so.

Though, if he wandered through the wrong parts of Springfield there was a chance the Latin Kings would just solve my problem for me... no, no. I didn't know if conventional weapons would even be able to harm Tzmir, and I'm sure Decca would have no end of insulting rhetoric for me if I just let Tzmir become the urban underclass's problem. I'd gotten myself in to this situation by taking the easy route, and I'd have to get myself out by taking the Mass Pike.

"Sounds like it's definitely a plan, then," I said. "But I don't know what we'll be able to do to record your, uh, your event. Ian, do you guys think you'd be able to follow them *all the way* to Springfield with your cameras?" I tried asking in a tone that implied an elbow-nudge, hoping that Tzmir came from a dimension where they had less ability to discern nuance than myself. Ian apparently did—he just flashed me an 'okay' gesture with a free hand while he was filming the group of Dagons. They were crouched in a circle, eating pizza and cardboard box fragments with equal enthusiasm.

"Capturing my act of ecstatic creation on video would be appreciated, but ultimately will be a mere formality. All shall be able to witness and, perhaps for small money, *cavort* in my aesthetically-ebullient estate. Men will assemble in an orderly queue prior, and in a frantic mob afterwards as they vie to pay tribute to my bold, dynamic vision!"

"Oh, of course. Wouldn't want mere technical difficulties to hold you back!" I cast a worried glance at Ian, but he was busy instructing Lumberjack to lie down in the middle of the Dagons' feeding area so he could film it. Someone collapsing on top of their pizza naturally ruined their interest in it, and Ian then had to skirt around the swiftly-disbanding circle trying to goad them back in to position.

"I'll have concluded my magnetic recitations by nightfall. Return then with the necessary plastic balls—you as my patron should be among the chosen few to witness the full unfolding of my corporeal largesse, Gregwithers!"

"Naturally! I wouldn't miss it for all the cans of 'Gansett in Amherst." I gave Tzmir a parting wave and walked over to Ian, who was sitting on a bench, fiddling with his camera. The Dagons resumed feeding, and Lumberjack was in my office with the door shut, presumably changing into pizza-free clothes.

"We'll be back with *something* tonight before it's time for them to do whatever they do with the moon," I whispered.

"If you aren't, then as soon as they look like they're starting up some kind of magic coven-circle, I'm turning this gallery into the Crazy World of Arthur Brown."

"Deal," I said, then hurried out of the gallery and away from the group of weird monsters who neither minded pineapple on their pizza, nor minded pizza on their cardboard boxes.

Decca called shotgun in my absence, which I think was against the rules, but it was hardly the right time to argue about such matters; and after a bracing trip through a Dunkin' Donuts drive-thru window we were on the Mass Pike heading towards Ripton.

"Now just keep going 70 until we get to the Sturbridge exit," Decca said, reading off of the directions we'd printed out.

"413 nothing, this guy is barely west 'a Woostah," said Myra.

Verrick did happen to live in what most people considered to be one of the less worth-going-to swaths of the state. Western Mass had the Berkshires and the Six-College area; the East had Boston and Cape Cod, and Salem and Arkham for the tourists; all that really lay between them was a lot of abandoned factories, sporadic apple orchards, and middling hills that weren't impressive enough to be counted as part of the Appalachias. All of Ripton and its surrounding towns were, to many of the state's residents, a stretch of land placed in between them and New Hampshire's fireworks, specifically to make them that much more frustrating to obtain. It seemed fitting that a recluse would live in a town that people were only interested in passing through without acknowledgment.

"So," I said after we'd left the radius of any of Decca's radio presets, "is an antinatalist some kind of art movement? Like the Surrealists?"

"Not necessarily," said Decca. "But if he goes out of his way to promote himself as such, he probably makes a point of creating things in that philosophical vein. The actual term means that he isn't too keen on people, both individually and as a concept."

"What kind of paintings does this guy make, anyways? I don't know that I'm familiar with his work," said Myra.

"He's nooon-representaaationaaal," Decca said, accompanied by a snide fluttering of her hands.

"He kind of makes... things that look like a cross between transit maps and a doctor's signature, but more structured; then there are little flourishy-bits on some places," I said.

I heard paper sliding around in the back, then Myra held her notebook up in between the front seats.

"Something sort of like this?"

We were on a straight section of highway at that point, so I glanced at it. There was, on the bottom half of the blue-lined page, a jumble of weirdly-angled lines that looked like a rough rendition of the very painting her statue had destroyed.

Above it was a Sharpie drawing of a scowling person with a thick black "V" of hair falling across their face, but I assumed that was unrelated.

"That's pretty accurate, yeah."

Decca peered over the top of the page and giggled. Myra quickly drew the notebook back.

"That design is something from the Miskatonic rejects I used to hang out with back when. So it looks like we might be on the right track with this guy."

We passed through a stretch of roadside cliff faces that used to be the insides of some rolling hills until someone decided that they were in a turnpike's way. I'd thought, as a kid, the thin tunnels in the cliffs were the burrows of some sort of tiny mountain-creature—instead of just man-made routes for dynamite. At that point, in light of the enormous aquatic creatures emerging from paintings and roving gangs of fishmen traveling over from the Cape to see them, it didn't really seem too implausible of a theory.

I considered saying as much, though thought I'd already been the butt of enough unwitting humor the last few days. Fortunately, Myra broke the silence again.

"Is that a lock through your ear?"

"Yep," said Decca. "Had it there since college."

"Did you throw away the key? Is it like one of those locks on that bridge in Paris?"

"No, I just lost it because my dorm was as tidy as anybody's dorm is freshman year. It doesn't *symbolize* anything, like a Navy dude I've promised to wait for. Just looks more bad ass than a stud."

In the rear view mirror I saw Myra idly rub the side of her nose, where she'd had a nose ring last year before she decided it felt like a cheap affectation.

There was another idle rustling of paper from the backseat, followed by a single chortle.

"It figures you'd have a collection of those Alice Alter zines, though a Vans box in the back of your car is hardly archival-quality storage."

"Those are for distribution," I said.

"Quiet, you," said Decca.

"What? Wait, do you work with her?"

Decca sighed, and slid lower in her seat. "Kind of."

Myra pulled the box out of the foot well and began rifling through it on the seat beside her. Decca glared at me as though I'd just unplugged a guitarist's amp mid-song.

"So, hah, Myra, what do you think Verrick might be able to do for us? Magically, I mean," I said.

"I don't even know. All my knowledge of it came from my old college friends, and who knows if they even knew what they were doing."

##

We eventually got off of the Mass Pike at the Sturbridge Village exit after collectively scouring Decca's car floor and cup holders for exact change at the tollbooth. We got on to I-Ninety-Three North, which took us through Stotham, Leominster, and eventually deposited us in Ripton. I could tell we were getting deep in to the hill towns, because the occasional roadside Cumby's were replaced by run-down equivalents with names like Athol Servicemart. We were out beyond the reach of franchises.

If we weren't passing through at high noon, it probably would have seemed as creepy and portentous as you'd expect it to be. I mean, in books and movies you'd expect the guy responsible for bringing ancient unspeakable horror into this world to live somewhere that's all hooting owls and gnarled old trees with faces in their bark, but it was a rather pleasant drive, truth be told. Even if the seemingly endless birch trees and hillside thickets did get a little samey after the first fifteen minutes.

When we found Verrick's street, we were glad it had a modern white-on-metallic-green sign rather than a faded panel of rotting wood.

Verrick's house was, as befitted a proper recluse, down quite a long, tree-ensconced driveway, which doubled back on itself a couple times for no apparent reason. We could see the house more distinctly through the thinning layers of trees as we approached, and it was definitely an old New England sort of affair. Square-ish, gambrel roof, multiple chimneys, wrap-around porch. I couldn't tell if it was actually painted a drab brownish-gray color or if it had just faded to that due to lack of upkeep.

Myra asked if anybody could count how many gables it had, which was met with snickering.

"I was almost expecting it to be a shoddy tenement housing unit surrounded by derelict manufacturing plants," said Decca, "that's my idea of modern middle-Massachusetts aesthetic."

"He sounds like the sort of fellow who'd run shrieking from any bit of modernity," said Myra.

"A Manifestian?" I said.

"Small 'm' modern," said Myra.

The driveway didn't end so much as it just blended in to the grass of the front lawn. I stopped the car on what didn't look like a particularly landscaped patch at the front of the house. We all got out of the car and ascended the porch steps, which gave a discomforting scale of creepy-old-house creaks. Myra edged behind Decca when we reached the top and were staring down the door.

"Do you have your club-whip thing with you? Just in case," she asked.

"My baton's in the car. What, do you want me to hit the *house*?"

I stood at arm's length, as a precaution, and reached out to ring the doorbell.

There was a fairly normal electronic chiming from behind the door. I heard some light commotion inside and eventually the doorknob clicked, turned, and the door opened on to what might have been the most nondescript person I've ever seen.

I don't mean just because you expect artists to be eccentric and wacky-looking, but even by college republican standards Donald Verrick was severely white-bread. His hair styled like one of those pictures on the wall at SuperCuts, which was that non-outstanding shade of brown that would be described as 'mousey' if he were a bookish woman. His facial features were in a ratio where none of them particularly stood out from the rest, though they all gave off a sense of slight annoyance. He'd probably manage to be five-nine both with and without shoes. His polo shirt was the same non-color as his hair.

"I presume that you're Greg Withers," he said.

"Well, one of us is," I said, followed by an attempt at a few cheery laughs that quickly died off when they weren't returned. "I am, yes; this is my vice-chairperson Decca, and our colleague Myra, who seems to know what the kind of thing it is that you do. The antinatalist art."

I was briefly surrounded by polite sighing.

"Mr. Withers, I have deduced from the obsequious news report that you have a Great Old One in your art gallery who is communing with the local Deep One population."

"I think those words describe the situation that we're in, yes."

"Then please come in, the three of you," he said, opening the door fully and stepping aside. "Wipe your feet, or don't. All is mere dust on a cosmic scale either way."

10

We entered Verrick's house, wiping our feet despite his impassiveness, and he led us through an oddly-wallpaper-patterned hallway into a living room that didn't quite seem to warrant that name. It was outfitted with a living room set my father would have scoffed at- a couch and love seat upholstered in a rough burnt-orange fabric with erratic stitches of contrasting color scattered across. A coffee table of plain off-yellow wood that was mottled with countless circular mug-stains. It was the sort of shabbiness you'd sooner expect to see in a library than a household. Decca and I took the couch; Myra took the loveseat catty-corner with the coffee table.

"I know you've driven some time to get here," Verrick said after we'd sat down. "And as the host of this meeting it would be polite of me get you some coffee or tea." That was distinctly a statement rather than a question, and he didn't wait around for us to request one or the other before he left through a door that appeared to lead to the kitchen, or at least a room that appeared to be coated entirely in Formica and melamine.

The inside of Verrick's house seemed as difficult to pin a specific style on as the man himself. Outside of the overdone kitchen, there was an ornately carved grandfather clock in the front hall, and the living room had a TV set with rabbit ears still affixed perched on a small folding table against the wall opposite our couch. There were a few picture frames scattered about the walls, though the pictures they contained didn't seem to be of anything in particular. One was simply the vacant driveway of a house that wasn't his. Another held a Polaroid slightly too small for the frame that seemed to just be an out-of-focus group of people.

"I really don't get a good vibe off of this guy," Decca whispered to me. "What's his angle in all this, his helping us?"

"Benevolence?" I said.

"He doesn't carry himself like a benevolent kind of guy. Or sound like one."

"Yeah, he comes across as an oddball, but I don't know that I'd trust advice in the field of magick from somebody who seemed socially well-adjusted," said Myra.

"Could be why yours didn't work."

Verrick brought out a tray with four mugs from the kitchen and set it on the table. Each of them was different, like you'd see in an office break room that had been accruing leftover dishes from decades of employee turnover. I chose the Garfield mug. As he'd said, it was filled with something that could have been either coffee or tea. I held it before me and took a sniff, the results of which were inconclusive, then set it on the table before me hoping he wouldn't notice if I never actually sipped from it.

He pulled up a hard plastic chair; the sort you'd find in an elementary school, to the table across from the couch.

"So," he began. "In an effort to not re-cover familiar

ground: what exactly do you three already know about the Eldritch underpinnings of New England?

"I have no idea what you mean," I said.

"I have no idea what you're referring to but I do know what those individual words mean, thank you very much," said Decca. Verrick seemed unfazed by her standoffishness.

"A few years back, I was friends with some people who'd transferred over from Misky U. We tried to do the whole summoning circle thing a few times, graved up a bunch of sigils —nothing like on the level that you do—even went up to Vermont for a weekend and played with waxed paper kazoos in the woods after dark. Nothing ever came of it, though, we were really just going through the motions. We might as well have been Wiccans for all the magick we were able to do."

Verrick folded his hands in his lap.

"So you are dimly aware that the universe is subject to the will of... beings... whose aims are antithetical to human life, should they chance to notice us at all."

"That's kind of a cornerstone of modern philosophy," said Decca.

"It should be understood that I speak in a more literal— and littoral—sense than philosophers tend to. Your betentacled visitor should attest to that."

"How did you know it was made of tentacles?" I said.

"They all are, to some extent. I'm a mere hobbyist when it comes to studying these occult matters and am not entirely proficient in their teratology. Though I can tell you of their methodology." He patted his chest, then his pants pockets, looked briefly more despondent than normal, then continued. "The planes of existence in which the Old Ones naturally reside are not entirely coterminous with our three spatial and one temporal dimension. It's a situation rather akin to CMYK color printing when one color's application is misaligned. Imprecise attempts to align some tunnel between the two, or send or receive some signal, will be perceived offset from their intended areas of effect, spatially or temporally. If your Arkham friends' dabbling did have any effect, due to their inexperience, it likely occurred some distance away, or could occur on the correct spot years from now.

"Treebridge, Massachusetts, you must understand, is a very imprecise signal."

Myra furrowed her brow and tilted her head.

"I don't follow you," Decca said.

"The settlement of the Massachusetts Bay Colonies began on the East coast with Plymouth, Kingsport and the like. Then it moved West. Arkham was already established and well on its way to becoming what it's now infamous for by the time that the Pioneer Valley was being settled and built up, and certain powerful individuals from the established parts of the state were able to exert their influence on nascent civil planners. You're familiar with the linear motifs I use in my paintings?"

"Oh yeah, they're wicked awesome," I said, with my vowels instinctively flattening for those two words.

Myra opened her notebook and showed her old drawing to Verrick. "Something like this?"

He studied the page for a moment then actually appeared to smile, though it was one of those off-putting kinds, which didn't engage the eyes. "I do not recognize that individual, though the diagram beneath it is very in line with my work for the Local Art Gallery. And it had not occurred to you what you have there?"

"I copied it from a Xerox one of the old gang had allegedly made from a secret forbidden tome in the University library's off-record archives."

"There are any number of books from which you could have made a passable facsimile of that diagram," Verrick said with a touch of amusement in his voice. He reached over, took the notebook from Myra, and laid it down on the coffee table. Then he traced a finger along one of the lines passing through the middle of the drawing. "Redfern," he said. He traced his finger along another. "Main, curling off in to Pleasant when it reaches the old train tunnel."

The three of us shared a moment of dawning realization. I wasn't going to break the silence for fear of presuming wrong, but fortunately Decca did by muttering, "Ya fahkin' kiddin' me."

"I was tracing... bus routes?" said Myra.

Verrick's smile increased by perhaps two degrees.

"Treebridge's downtown area was intended to serve as a massive sigil for the calling of an extraplanar entity. Specifically, the one currently holding court in your gallery.

"It has been attempted elsewhere in the state, to varying degrees of success. Some believe the curious atavism noted among certain old Tarbox families to be the result of a particularly insidious landscaper, and there are some worrying alignments of curlicues when one views the silhouettes of Six Flags' roller coasters from certain angles, though as if intentional their purpose has yet to be realized. But the intertwining of Treebridge's major streets creates, to close enough extent, a summoning sigil.

"There are inconsistencies in the 'grammar,' of course. A few curlicues that a hill's slope may have prevented the proper rendering of. The need to skew around property they couldn't obtain legal right to pave over. And of course mere human error in calculation. But the cumulative effect is that the lines they *actually* put down would summon the intended target some generations after it was intended to.

"The placing of my painting—another sigil—at a particular location within the larger one—such as your gallery— altered its form enough to prevent the entity from emerging. That is, until you removed it."

"It wasn't removed so much as, well, destroyed," I said,

avoiding looking at him as I did so.

"I knew there was something really off about this area," said Decca, "but I thought it was just the influx of hipsters." She leaned forward, over the table. "Do you think it's summoning them, too? Is there another magic pattern around the city that prevents the Puerto Ricans moving up from Holyoke and spoiling the homogeneity? Or is that just regular economics?"

"Decca, he's trying to help us," Myra said.

"I'm being serious, I'd love there to be some magic thing we could just dispel and suddenly there's a solid labor force in the city."

"Mock me if it permits you to cope with the intrusion of non-anthropocentric forces in to your cosmological Weltanschauung, but they will intrude regardless of your flippancy. I had tried what I could in order to staunch their incursion to our plane, but as my efforts have proved insufficient, I have decided to simply resign myself to the erasure of this manikin existence which their arrival portents."

"I beg your pardon," I said, getting neither the intent of his last statement nor the precise words he'd used in it.

"He doesn't see the point in helping us because we're all gonna die," said Decca. "Figures we'd get saddled arguing with a nihilist." She crossed her arms and slouched back against the couch.

"Mr. Verrick, this creature isn't trying to devour our souls. I think it's more interested in conceptual art."

"It was merely a coincidence that it appeared in your gallery," he said. "I would not advise you read anything in to that. Their cognitive processes are as beyond our comprehension as ours would be to stoats and voles."

"Oh no, this thing has actually said that it wants to make a splash in the art world," I said.

"I assure you the Old Ones are not concerned with anything so quotidian as local culture."

"This one is, though," said Myra.

"It told us so. At length. We actually heard the words straight from what I've assumed is its mouth," I said.

"I don't know what kind of Elder Starfucks you've actually spoken with, but the one we're in negotiation with has a lot more real-world implications than you're willing to cop to," said Decca.

I'd say Verrick looked unfazed at her remark, but I'm not entirely sure what faze would even look like on his face. He could have made a killing on the professional poker circuit if they'd put up with his vocabulary.

A corner of his mouth twitched slightly.

"I don't presume it could simply have been trying to lull you into a false sense of security?"

"Why would something that size need to be conniving?" said Decca.

He nodded, and adjusted his posture in his rather uncomfortable-looking chair. "Well, if true, then I suppose I am not sympathetic to this particular Old One's plans."

"So you'll help us get rid of this thing?" I said.

"To the extent that I am capable, yes."

"Are you actually a full-fledged magician?" said Myra. "I had tried to banish or unbind or whatever the thing in the gallery with what I think were spells from the old college days." She began leafing through her notebook.

"I'm not so proficient in the more esoteric practices," said Verrick. "I merely have a recreational interest in the dire truths which underpin reality, and find that certain magical practices dovetail nicely with my painting hobby."

"So you can make a painting that will get rid of the creature?"

"Given some time I can prepare a sigil to reseal the portal from which the creature has emerged, yes."

"Thank you," I said.

"You're talking around her question," said Decca. "Is that going to get rid of the big gribbly thing?"

"It will prevent any further things from emerging through the portal once it's in place, though I'm afraid I have no capability to rid you of the creature that has already emerged."

There was one of those hear-a-pin-drop pauses.

"I might recommend an elephant gun," he added.

Decca merely threw her head back over the top of the couch.

"Are you serious?" said Myra.

"You know we're talking about a fifteen-foot tall gorilla-shaped lobster with a face made of bad anime that wants to do whatever the hell it pleases?" I said.

"I am aware of their general appearance, yes."

"And there's still the matter of the.... the Deep Ones, did you call them? The fish people that Tzmir has called over to attend to him," Myra said.

Verrick steepled his fingers before his mouth for a moment. "I'm sure that managing to kill the larger one would serve to demoralize the Deep Ones and send them running back to the Quabbin."

I heard another metaphorical pin drop, followed by a trio of *whats* from the three of us. Verrick seemed, again, amused by our confusion.

"You had assumed it was just a reservoir. I assure you, it's one of the more... colourful... sites in central Massachusetts."

Decca looked sickened, Myra cradled her head in her hands. I simply sat there, jaw agape like the sea-things whose natural habitat we'd apparently all been drinking from.

"You're fucking with us now," said Myra.

"That was perhaps unfair and unnecessary of me. I shouldn't overburden you with extraneous revelation when there are more immediate matters to deal with." He rose from his chair and checked his watch. "If you're willing to display a less-elaborate painting in your gallery which will sufficiently seal the portal, then I can perhaps prepare and deliver one in a matter of hours."

I leaned over the armrest to see the face of the grandfather clock down the hall. "That would be perfect, actually. Tzmir said it needed to wait until the moon came out to finish emerging from its portal, so you have the whole afternoon to do what you've got to do."

Verrick nodded. "The portal will have to be vacant before it can be sealed, you realize. Same as closing a door, just functioning on planes we're not equipped to perceive."

"We need to kill this thing *and* dispose of the body?" asked Decca.

"You're awfully fixated on murdering this thing," Myra said. "We can maybe, I don't know, come up with a convincing argument to dissuade it from its original plan. We have time."

"Hello? Radical left activist, here. If rigorous and sensible arguments were able to accomplish anything then we'd actually be a potent political force outside of Vermont town hall meetings. If someone wants to invade a thing you can't just argue them out of it."

"It's worth a try," I said. "I'd rather prefer that we went with a method that didn't risk spilling that thing's possibly weirdly-chemicalled blood all over the building. It looks like the sort of thing you'd expect to have acid blood. Do they?"

"It's a possibility. Acid, toxicity, mutagenic properties... perhaps their blood itself possesses a separate sentience—a different failed organism whose life-functions have been bent to the stronger creature's ends." Verrick looked off in to the middle distance with what actually seemed to be vague awe in his eyes momentarily, then regained his composure and shrugged. "Your guess would be as good as mine, really."

"Heck of a consultant you are," Decca said.

"I am still offering to solve more of your predicament than you would be able to on your own, as evidenced by your past failings. And do take in to account that I have not brought up the subject of financial remuneration for my damaged painting."

"You are—he is—" I said as I leaned in between the two of them. Decca leaned back on the couch and crossed her arms. "Look, Mr. Verrick, we're incredibly thankful that you're willing to help us like this, it means the world to us."

"An... appropriate choice of words," he said, along with an exhalation that might have been a try at a laugh.

"So, you can get another painting to the gallery by this evening?"

"Most certainly. I have several canvases prepared already, and there is little in the way of temperamental artistic inspiration involved in these sigils."

"Excellent. We should get going and decide on our end of the plan, but, we'll expect you for sundown?"

"Sundowning is the most you can expect out of that dude," Decca said when we got into the car and were safely out of earshot.

"What is that even supposed to mean?" I asked, as I navigated back through Verrick's twisty driveway.

"Guy's a tool."

"He's helping us get rid of the portal in the gallery," said Myra.

"Which is the *easy* part. All he's got to do is push some tempera paint around while we're still at square one. When it comes to the more immediate problem of stopping Tzmir from doing anything that involves the outside world, we're on our own"

"We still have about eighty miles on the Pike in which to figure that out," I said.

"Fuck, not even an hour."

"Come on. We're three resourceful and roughly-college-educated folks, we can brainstorm this," said Myra. She flipped open her notebook and produced a pen from the slurry of items on the car's back seat. "So, big alien torso sitting in the gallery and scheming with some smaller aliens."

"The Deep Ones aren't aliens," I said, "Verrick told us that they live—"

"Humanoid. Aliens. From *beyond the stars* alright? In the gallery. We have the three of us and a collapsible baton."

Decca slapped the dashboard. "We've got the car. The gallery has that big storefront window. We could drive this thing right through the glass and just squash it up against the wall."

"Can we try to come up with a Plan A that involves significantly *less* property damage than letting Ian torch the place?" I said.

"There are less drastic solutions than that, I'm sure of it," said Myra. "What exactly was it that Tzmir said it wanted to do? Can we work off of that?"

"Make art that nobody is going to appreciate. Reveal his existence to the world at large and probably turn a bunch of other people in to gibbering wrecks while doing so."

"Okay. What can we do to discourage it from wanting to be an artist?"

"Tell it there's no money in it," said Decca.

"I don't think it would really grasp the importance of that," I said.

"It's an overcrowded market and the odds of getting noticed for all your efforts among the sea of competitors are astoundingly low," said Myra. "Though I assume Tzmir wouldn't really have a problem standing out among the rest of the art world being a giant monster and all. Next argument? How about 'what will your parents think?'"

"Hm, an appeal to emotion? Do whatever it is actually have parents?" said Decca.

None of us could come up with a viable answer to that.

"Well that might not be totally off the table depending on biology," Myra said. "We have a maybe; that's progress."

"Glad someone can be optimistic about all this" Decca said. "You weren't at all the other night."

"I mean, yeah, I wasn't then, but thinking about Verrick just... it kinda showed me ways that I don't want to be."

"Hey, how do you not get beaten down by the questions we're trying to sink Tzmir with? Sorry if that's personal or anything."

"Just stubborn idealism, I guess. Combined with the fact that I'm pretty good at the technical aspects of art, no matter what that thing says."

"What other advice from parents and friends hasn't discouraged anybody in this car?" I said.

"How about telling Tzmir that it'll never be as good as insert-artist-it-admires?" said Myra.

"Ooh, yeah. It will always be in The Shadow Out of Time's shadow," said Decca.

"It does seem to be pretty vain, that might worth a try," I said.

"Then if that doesn't work, car," said Decca.

I got to give her the sort of glare she'd previously given me, but her smirk told me that's what she was trying to get out of me.

"Small explosives, then? I may or may not have a local source for some of those."

"Nothing that will send parts of things flying around the gallery please."

"Okayyy."

"Try telling it that Ian's both a successful artist and a douchebag and if it wants to be a successful artist then everybody's going to think it's a douchebag too," said Myra.

"I dunno," I said, "I don't think Tzmir would worry about that. Ian's holding its attention just by pretending to be himself."

"And the dude's totally on my side when it comes to killing the hell out of the thing, loath as I would otherwise be to defend him," said Decca.

"See, that's why just killing Tzmir is a bad idea, Ian's for it."

"You've certainly turned on him."

"He was totally trying to screw us over until Tzmir showed up and muscled him out of the spotlight."

Decca leaned her seat back to include Myra in the conversation, if awkwardly so. "You might have liked to know that he got a bit of the ol' existential dread when we brought him in to the gallery. Maybe you artists are just hypersensitive to that sort of thing, like there's a little canary in your brain and Eldritch horrors are a mineshaft."

Myra shrugged. "Maybe that's what turned Verrick into the anti-Mister Rogers. He might have been a perfectly sociable person until he did too much abyss-staring and just gave in to the fear and trembling."

My phone chirped with a text message. We had enough potential things that could go wrong in our plans without risking my driving off the road into a ditch, so I handed the phone to Myra and told her to play secretary.

"Ian says there are people outside the gallery with signs protesting the filming that they think is taking place."

"Oh, bother... ask him just how many people he means."

Myra typed up the question. After about a minute, there was a response.

"Just five or six, he says."

It chirped again.

"What does, 'Bastardholes from Sunday with the stickers are back,' mean?"

"Of course it would be them again."

"Hey! How do you think they'd handle being introduced to Tzmir and the Deep Things?" said Decca.

I don't know if she was being facetious, but I actually found myself giving that a moment's thought.

"I mean, if our plan is really going to be trying to just *complain* Tzmir out of existence, then they definitely have enough experience for the job."

"Yeah, discouragement is their bag. Rope them in and art-shame Tzmir into submission, then stop them from shaming before Verrick gets there because, wow, he doesn't even have enough spoons as it is," said Decca.

"We can't be sure that they won't just go and blab about what we did to anybody."

"Who are they going to tell and what's illegal about it?" asked Myra.

"I... I don't know. It just really feels like the kind of thing the authorities don't want you doing."

"I don't think I've ever heard of anybody getting arrested for dabbling in dark magic stuff, and I know from unjust arrests," said Decca.

"I think most of the folks you hear about doing it are too dead or insane to arrest afterwards."

"Oh boy."

"Shut up with that. Optimism. We're doing this," said Myra. "Plan A: De-escalation. Plan B?"

"Plan B: Collapsible baton," said Decca, unsheathing it for display.

"Fine. After an exhaustive attempt at Plan A, we get physical. And if that doesn't work then we let Ian burn it to the ground."

"Underline 'exhaustive' in your notes, please," I said.

We scrounged enough quarters from the nooks of Decca's car to get a spot in the public lot until 5:58 PM, and we figured that if we couldn't get back to it in the two minutes between the meter expiring and the lot becoming free for the night, then it would be because we had a bigger problem on our hands than a parking ticket. I was secretly holding out for it getting a boot put on it so that Plan B, if it came down to that, would be significantly smaller in scale than our original ideas.

We made our way up the hill towards the gallery, Myra with her notebook, me with some pages of notes to go off of torn from her notebook, and Decca with her baton tucked into her waistband; and for all I knew a snub-nose gun hidden in her boot and a shard of linoleum tile sewn into the hem of her sweater.

There were, as Ian had reported, six Manifestians standing on the sidewalk outside of the gallery. The city still had the ends of the street barricaded to accommodate Ian's film shoot, and while the sidewalks weren't guarded by police or cordoned off with tape it still looked unwelcoming, so people seemed dissuaded from walking down the street and there was nobody really around to pay attention to their protest.

We were noticed practically as soon as we stepped on to the street by the smaller Manifestian who I recognized as the culprit in the ladder tug-of-war that started this whole thing. He broke from the group carrying his little sign, which read "WON'T REIFY EFFUSIVE CINEMATIC DERELICTION," and scampered over to presumably try and form a barrier or just scamper around us waving his sign. Though once he got within a couple feet there was a sharp *shink* sound followed by a *thwip*, then he fell to the ground holding his calf. I stopped and looked over at Decca, who was trying to slide her recollapsed baton into a hip pocket. Something in its latching mechanism mustn't have caught right, however, and it sprung back out. The sudden force caused her to stagger sideways into Myra and the baton launched itself a few meters down the street where it proceeded to bounce end-over-end a few times, before skittering onto a storm drain and falling in.

The rest of the Manifestians turned to see me standing among three fallen howling people; two with laughter, one with whooping breaths that were close enough to pass for laughing at a distance. Probably not the most dramatic entrance one can make, but a memorable one nonetheless. I greeted them with a wave.

"You again," shouted the weirdly-facial-haired leader of the group.

I knelt to help Myra and Decca to their feet and we finished our approach, stepping around the fellow Decca had charlie-horsed.

"Look," I said to the leader, "we don't have time for any of your Manifestian antics, there's a—"

"This is not a formal action on behalf of the.... fuck it, the Manifestians. There's been internal disagreement over the ideological direction of this issue and we're acting as a splinter faction, WRECD."

Decca groaned in response.

"We don't have time for your stupid artistic hair splitting, but if you want to make an actual difference in something for a change, we have what will hopefully be a once-in-a-lifetime opportunity waiting for you inside the gallery."

The leader tilted his head, examining me for a moment.

"We'll not parlay with the enemy," shouted one of the other sign-holders.

"Wait. You actually want us to engage in open debate?" said the leader.

"In a manner of speaking, yes."

There was a stunned silence from the rest of the group, then someone whispered, "What do we do?"

Their leader had the bold smile of someone expecting the precise opposite of what somebody else has planned for them.

"Alright, let's go."

"Just you, though," said Myra, "none of the rest."

"I'm sure I can hold my own."

Decca locked an arm around one of his and turned him to face the gallery, then gestured for Myra to take the other arm. "Just in case, though."

I knocked on the gallery door, waited for a response, then texted Ian when there wasn't one. After another moment the door unlocked, and we were ushered in.

11

The Deep Ones were all over near a power outlet on the wall nearest the door, huddled around Ian's laptop and a small clutch of microphones that were plugged in to it. Ian was sitting at the desk in my office, with one of his cameras on the desk that looked to be plugged in to my computer, and he was apparently doing something with the two. Tzmir was in its usual place, with its elbows on the floor, hands steepled before it, looking as pleased as something without the capacity to smile can. And our Manifestian was slouched in Decca and Myra's arms screaming his head off practically as soon as Lumberjack closed the door.

There was frantic knocking from the others outside the gallery when their leader started screaming. Lumberjack knocked back with the flat of his palm and shouted, "Hot set, keep it down! Filming in progress!" Then he turned to the Manifestian inside. "Chill, dude."

Our dude did not chill.

Decca and Myra shared an annoyed glance and released their arms, dropping him on his butt. He stopped screaming with an oddly-childlike hiccup upon impact to just sit rigid and gawping, like an indoors-only cat that had escaped out onto the lawn and had no idea how to come to terms with the existence of the sky.

Ian appeared in the doorway of the office with a look of concern on his face. Tzmir turned his attention to our little group, sans facial expression.

"It's quite fortunate that we were not actively recording at the time of your entrance, but I must confess confusion as to why you felt my project would benefit from another Crying One. Ianirvin, is that another one of your people? I thought they had all been familiarized with our activities by now."

I turned to Ian and tried to discreetly make no-shut-up-secret gestures with my hands. He observed the scene and myself for a moment with appropriate confusion.

"I... guess he must have just forgotten! You know how flighty those artist folks can be, eh?" He waved us over to the office. "We'll get him cooled off."

Lumberjack grabbed the Manifestian around the shoulders, Decca took his legs, and they carried him over to the office with Myra and I. Ian shut the door behind us. It was rather cramped with all six of us in my office, and we wound up standing in a circle around my desk after Lumberjack propped the Manifestian against the wall in a corner next to the bag of plastic balls.

Ian stood with his arms straight, both hands palm-down on the desk. "So, you guys haven't brought anything to help. Are we getting our burn on or what?"

"We've brought two things to help put an end to it all," I said. "One of them will be arriving just around sundown and the other is unexpectedly catatonic. But, we have a backup."

"You better have a good Plan B, 'cause we can get going right here right now on Plan F if you don't."

"I'm Plan B," I said. I took advantage of the opportunity to draw a handful of folded papers out of my own pocket for a change. It really did feel authoritative. "We have the gist of what he was going to say right here, and I can prattle it off with fewer cusses than Decca would."

Something between a sigh and a giggle came out of the Manifestian. Lumberjack sidled over, knelt beside him, and patted him on the cheek. "You back with us, bro?"

His face slowly bobbed over to meet Lumberjack's, though his expression was still vacant. Lumberjack grabbed a couple of colorful balls from out of the bag next to them and waved them around in front of his face. The Manifestian's eyes tracked the balls, and he *ooohed* softly.

We watched the two of them briefly, then when nothing seemed to be coming from it, we returned to the conversation at hand.

"We're going to persuade Tzmir that the art world may not be the best outlet for his particular abilities," said Myra.

"You're going to play the concerned parents and try talking it into choosing a different major? Is that all?"

"Yes," I said.

"That's fucking it?"

"I did do a pretty good number on you when I was hungover the other day," I said, though my confidence in the plan had begun flagging at that last remark.

"Greg has twenty minutes to browbeat that thing and then we try hitting it with a car," said Decca.

Ian's face lit up at hearing that and he clasped his hands together before him.

"You. Are. A. Homeboy. Were you planning to drive it straight through the plate glass window up front?"

"Oh yeah. I can get enough speed coming up the hill and

just paste the bastard against the wall."

Ian stepped around the desk and gave Decca a hearty pat on the back, seemingly oblivious to the fact that she bristled at his doing so. "Y'know, Bratmobile, you really ain't so bad," he said to her with unusual warmth.

Ian then picked up his camera from the desk and tugged its USB cord out from the computer tower. "We're gonna go set up for a couple angles to get a really, really killer moneyshot of you plowing through the storefront while Greg does his thing."

I felt... I don't quite know how what to call it. I imagine a camel having its back broken with a straw would feel far more directly painful than what I felt, it was more like a worn rubber band that was being stretched around something too large had snapped.

"You're betting *against* me?" I said.

Ian paused partway out the office door with a hand-in-the-cookie-jar expression on his face.

"You don't think this is going to work and you're banking on getting more footage when it doesn't."

Ian's eyes darted around to everyone else's in the room, other than the Manifestian's, before anxiously returning to mine.

"Yeah, dude, sorry. It'd make for a lot better cinema." Then he slunk out the door.

Lumberjack stood up—and all of our gazes, other than the Manifestian's again, fixed on him. Along with the surprised expression he took on, his beard seemed to fluff out like an agitated cat's tail.

"Don't look at me, guys, he's the one in charge. I gotta go where the pay is." Then he followed Ian out of the office door.

My face was severely warm. I'd had plenty of reasons to think Ian was a complete weasel before then, but to have it thrown in my face like that was something else entirely. I felt like someone who had woken up from a pleasant lucid dream, only to discover that they'd drunk too much the previous evening and would spend the majority of the day paying for it.

I realized suddenly that I had it within me to do this.

"Oh my God," said the Manifestian as he seemed to be coming back to reality, "what the fuck have you Smithies done?"

After a short period of briefing our Manifestian on the situation we'd dragged him in to—which, in hindsight, we really should have done before entering the gallery—it was decided that he would be best put to use huddling in my office with his tail between his legs. There weren't any bananas left, but we figured he'd survive for the next twenty minutes until the building was no longer structurally sound and potentially on fire.

Decca, Myra, and I exited the office. Myra and I approached Tzmir, while Decca circled around and began shooing the Deep Ones to the other side of the gallery.

"Clear the way, go, vaminos," she said, making sweeping motions with her arms towards the other side of the gallery. "Got to make a clear shot here."

"We aren't gonna be filming over there," Ian called over, though Decca didn't acknowledge him. He and Lumberjack were each positioning a camera on a tripod on either side of the gallery's bay window, muttering about angles and lighting and whatnot.

Tzmir seemed to be looking around at all the things happening in the gallery. Its headkelp were fanned out. I ruffled the papers I was holding and cleared my throat to try and get its attention, but that was probably drowned out by the school of Deep Ones moving around us as I did so.

"Hey, Tzmir," I said when they had passed.

"Gregwithers," it said. Its headkelp tightened and it leaned forward. "What exactly are the preparations that you have underway?"

"We're just trying to get some really solid, clean shots of you before you completely, uh, unfold, is it?"

Tzmir either nodded, or its headkelp were affected by an unseen breeze. I tried to muster up the physical sensation of the embarrassment I felt at letting myself get led on as I had been, and imagined Tzmir wearing a large version of Ian's goddamned corduroy blazer. It actually had a ridge of shell going around its upper body and neck area that somewhat resembled lapels, now that I thought about it.

"So yeah, before that happens, we just had a couple of reservations about the direction you're looking to go with your installation art project slash event-occurrences."

Tzmir flexed its back, and leaned on its forearms, and interwove its fingers on the floor in front of it. It clacked its claws in a brief little rhythm, as though just to draw our attention to the fact that it had them.

"I'm afraid it's a little too late in the planning process to offer any creative feedback."

"It's not so much your creativity, as the market for it that we're worried about," said Myra, with a distinctly softer 'good cop' tone in her voice.

"Yeah, we've done a little research, and it turns out that previous creative ventures by extraplanar entities haven't really drawn much of a paying audience. You've mentioned being familiar with Shub-Nigurath, right? Sure she's got a thousand young, but have you actually *seen* any? They don't get around, nobody's interested in them as anything more than a curiosity."

"Shub-Nigurath has always focused too much on quantity at the expense of quality, in my estimation. I'm not nearly so... so mass-market."

Decca passed between the two of us in a crouch, picking up the dribbly candles that were arranged around Tzmir.

"Even so," I said. "What kind of market penetration is your 'quality' really going to achieve?" I hoped my air-quotes stung. I hoped that Tzmir knew what air-quotes were. It did seem to have a decent grasp of human body language.

"Have you ever heard of a painter by the name of Richard Pickman?" said Myra.

"I can't say that I have," said Tzmir.

"That's exactly my point." I stood with my arms crossed over my chest, trying to imitate Ian's appearance of overconfidence. "The man had talent to spare back in his heyday, but where did it get him? You aren't going to come across his name in textbooks any time soon."

"There probably isn't even a memorial dorm wing at Misky U named for him," added Myra.

"You see, I'm putting a lot of money behind your creative venture here, and in case you aren't that familiar with how the film industry operates, the people fronting the money for your projects expect to see some return on their investment. Right, Ian?"

"Sure thing, seventeen minutes," Ian called across the gallery.

Tzmir clacked one of its claws sharply.

"I fail to see what you are getting at, Gregwithers, and I'm loath to give credence to anything the Crying One might have to say after her ineffectual... *propositioning* earlier."

Myra rolled her eyes, muttered, "take it away, couch boy," then wandered over to a bench near the huddled Deep Ones.

I took a deep breath and glanced down at my notes, mentally crossing off the previous bullet point and absorbing some of the bigger words for the one I was on. I told myself that the routine might work even better with just a bad cop. I closed my eyes and focused on feeling angry at my prior passivity for a second, then continued.

"I'm getting at the fact that there might be more prestigious and profitable—maybe even socially beneficial—things that I could be putting my money towards. What's your end goal, here? Nothing more than drawing as much attention to yourself as you can?"

At that, Tzmir formed its headkelp into a round-ish barrel shape and proceeded to rest its head in one of its large hands while emitting an exasperated, and oddly high-pitched, sigh.

"Oh, you short-sighted humans. Do you truly cling to your own limited perceptions of reality so adamantly? Your profit motives and economic systems. Your societal norms and concepts of propriety. All this conscious charade of yours leaves you unable to conceive of a truly transcendent art form."

"Myra, gimme a hand here," Decca called, "Ian says this stuff's gotta go." She had hefted one end of a length of scaffolding from the pile that lay off to Tzmir's right, my left. Myra looked at Ian, who wasn't paying any attention to our side of the gallery, then shuffled over to help.

Tzmir continued in its more ominous mode: "When I enact my special plan later this evening—and that's a when, mind you, not an if—then monetary gain will cease to be a factor in your existence."

"It will definitely cease to be a factor when I don't have any, because I blew it all on trying to make a documentary about an—" I struggled for concision with my venom "—an unproven hack-job. What makes you think anybody's even going to care about a fucking abandoned property converted into a ball pit? Even if you tell people that you upcycled the balls from a Chuck E. Cheese dumpster and glue some pinecones and old shoes to the outside of the house because hey, fuck it, against all odds found art is still a thing."

Tzmir drummed its fingers with its free hand.

"Is that the end of your tirade? Because I assure you that further words along similar lines will have just as little impact." Tzmir bunched its headkelp together tightly, then spread them wide and covered them with its hand as it emitted what could only have been an enormous yawn. "Which is to say nothing of the fact that you seem incapable of interpreting my intentions."

For all the vitriol I'd brought to bear, I felt again like I was being outmaneuvered. I decided, since there seemed to be far more than my reputation at stake in this, to double down.

"All you have to interpret is the same unfounded sense of self-worth that any of those applications that you just up and stole an idea from had!"

"A much more palatable way to worm my way into the public consciousness, don't you think? I was frankly surprised to find that none prior to myself had considered such a mundane delivery vector for the madness we prefer to sow wherever we manifest in your dimensions. The others have all resorted to taking the direct approach; it's so tacky, wearing their intentions on their sleeves like that. But I'll break new ground by working my madness through sheer inanity! No revelation of horrible hidden histories—indeed, the revelation will be that beyond the veil lie not secret vistas but more of the very same thing one seeks to escape from. A creeping insanity born of perpetual familiarity! And I won't need your financial approval to enact—"

Tzmir's monologue was then cut off by a large brass spire getting driven into its chest with a bile-raising crack as it pierced through the shell, held around its base by Decca and Myra. I hadn't even registered their beginning to do something like that—out of the corner of my vision they had just seemed to be moving Ian's pile of equipment.

The Deep Ones began croaking and gurgling amongst themselves, and Ian let out a suitably loud curse. Tzmir reeled back from the impact of their improvised art-lance and emitted another high-pitched shriek in that bizarre register it used when it first emerged from the wall; and its claws snapped frantically. It grabbed the statue with both of its larger hands and struggled to pull it out, as Decca and Myra tried to force it in further, though their shoes seemed unable to get enough traction on the hardwood floor. Decca lost her grip and stumbled forward onto her hands and knees, causing Myra to drop their end of the statue and run to help her up. Tzmir lurched forward slightly, but seemed to realize it couldn't go further without driving the brass spike deeper in with the way it was angled against the ground. I thought I heard an *oh dip* come from Ian's direction.

"What," Tzmir gasped, "was that for, you—" then it either retched or called them several derogatory names in the Deep Ones' language.

Decca and Myra looked at each other quizzically for a moment. I certainly didn't have any explanation to offer Tzmir, I was busy watching the pooling blood on the floor to see if it was going to start fizzing or anything.

"I think the artist's intentions were fairly unsubtle with that piece," said Decca.

It steadied its torso with one hand against the floor and pulled the statue straight out with the other, bringing a dark gout of ichor-that I really hoped wasn't acidic-foaming out with it. Decca and Myra shuffled back towards me as Tzmir furiously slammed the statue into the floor before them, then released it and slammed his fist down onto it, thoroughly crumpling it and probably doing a good amount of damage to the floor's finish. It then braced itself against the floor with both arms and pushed, forcing its lower body back through its portal nearly up to its armpits. The croaking from the Deep Ones seemed to grow more nervous.

"Like hell I'm going to grace your universe with my

presence after *that*," it said, then flattened a hand against its shell and slid it through the portal as well. The luminous purple border contracted around Tzmir's form as it vanished through the wall. Then it emitted an enormous retching sound, bent forward and from somewhere within its headkelp hocked an enormous wad of spit onto the gallery floor.

"Fuckers aren't worth my temporal motion," Tzmir said, then pulled the rest of itself back through the portal. The purple glow tapered around Tzmir's arm as it withdrew, middle finger last, and retracted down to a bright little speck on the wall, which either winked completely out of existence or was simply washed out by the gallery's overhead lighting.

The first ones to react to Tzmir's exit were the Deep Ones, who emitted a collective wail and made a mad rush for the front of the gallery. Ian and Lumberjack scrambled out of their path and Ian managed to grab one camera, but Gaknaugak grabbed the other and hurled it through the plate glass window, shattering it and letting most of the Deep Ones clamber through, though one was conscientious enough to simply kick the front door off its hinges and exit that way. A chorus of screams from outside signaled that the remaining Manifestians huddled outside the gallery were as dismayed by the situation as the Deep Ones were.

Ian shoved his camera into Lumberjack's hands and began shoving Lumberjack through the opened window.

"Follow them, dude! Go! Last chance for some good footage!"

"How far am I following 'em?"

"As far as you can! I don't care! Go!"

I turned from the scene back to Decca and Myra, who both looked as shocked by the whole thing as I felt. Then Decca took a deep breath, put a hand on Myra's shoulder, turned Myra towards her and leaned in with an open-mouthed kiss. They held for a few seconds, then Decca pulled away and said, "Sorry, adrenaline."

"Really shoulda asked, but it's not unwelcome," Myra said, and pulled her back to resume. Out of consideration, I turned on my heel and looked at one of the shadowboxes on the nearby wall. All the hanging exhibits, as far as I could tell, seemed to still be in place.

"HOLD UP DUDE GET THE CAMERA BACK HERE NOW," Ian called to Lumberjack out the window, after looking back in our direction.

The rest of the Manifestians had scattered in whichever directions the Deep Ones hadn't, but their leader hung around and helped us move the police barricades from out on the street to block the gallery's broken door and window. We stacked some of the scaffolding behind them too, for good measure, though that did run the risk of getting yet another piece of functional hardware mistaken for installation art.

A police car arrived shortly after the Deep Ones escaped, and Ian calmed the officers with some more film industry hand-waving. Some reporters arrived shortly after that and were treated to the same, but with more grandiose gesturing from Ian during the exchange. I was too busy helping block off the gallery when the exchanges were happening to overhear much, but they seemed to leave satisfied. At least, Ian seemed satisfied when he took up residence on a sidewalk bench to wait for Lumberjack's return afterwards. He'd also likely noticed that the Deep Ones' general aroma was still lingering inside the gallery, along with a sort of acridness that must have been from whatever it was that came out of Tzmir.

Probably two hours after we'd gotten back to the gallery, I was finally able to slump exhausted and jittery from the waning excitement at my office desk, and had no idea where to begin when it came to officially filing some sort of paperwork with some group for everything that had just happened. After I'd spent some time sitting there in a mental fog, Decca walked in. She leaned up against the doorjamb and ran a hand through her hair.

"I thought I'd had an idea to prevent too much property damage from happening. Sorry about that," she said.

"That wasn't really your fault. I do kind of wish you'd let me try another five minutes or so with Tzmir, though. I think I was finally starting to get my sea legs when it comes to assertiveness."

"Yeah, I know, but when we were moving that statue to make way for the car I found out it was hollow inside, and we were able to lift it easily enough, and the opportunity just sort of presented itself. At least we totally dashed Ian's hopes for a grand set piece."

That did cheer me up somewhat. As though the knowledge that we'd probably saved the world weren't enough.

"The Manifestian left, but I took down his contact info in case you need him as, I dunno, corroborating evidence or something," she said.

There was a knock on the doorframe, followed by Verrick peering around the corner. I quickly invited him in, and he was followed by Myra carrying a reproduction of his first painting with both hands, turning sideways through the door with it. He was wearing a surgical facemask over his nose and mouth, which I assumed was due to the smell that still filled the gallery, but nobody had spoken to him since we left Ripton, so that might just have been part of his normal attire when leaving the house.

"So we've preserved the state of unexamined manikin existence which we so prize," he said. "I gather that the concentrated disaster site against one wall would be the area in which the portal was to be found?"

"Yeah. There should still be some wires set up that you can hang the sigil from, unless those got torn down at some point in the last couple days. Is there still a ladder out there?"

"We moved one earlier, so yeah, there should be," said Decca.

"I have to admit that I was not all that confident in your ability to intimidate an Old One. What exactly did you do to eliminate the creature as a threat?" he said.

I felt it wouldn't really benefit anybody to let Verrick know that Tzmir was apparently just taking a roundabout route to being exactly what he thought it was, but that fact was easily glossed over with some shock and awe.

"We wound up just stabbing it until it went away," I said. "The weapon is lying in the puddle of phlegm and monster blood around the ruined canvas if you'd like to inspect it, but I don't know if any of that is toxic or infectious like we'd worried about earlier."

Verrick's eyes widened, and he actually stammered a bit before speaking. "I didn't, uh, I did some cursory research after our discussion and didn't find any indications of airborne pathogens originating from Old Ones."

"Excellent. I guess I'll get a cleaning crew in here tomorrow and you can just sort of step around it while setting the painting up."

He looked back at Myra, and the painting she was carrying across her body bobbed upwards to approximate a shrug.

"That we will do, and then we can discuss your remuneration for the original damaged work."

Verrick left the office with Myra in tow. Decca stayed behind. I must have looked as dismayed by the prospect of dealing with insurance as I actually felt, because a second after they left she said, "Hey, fahkin' A, right? We might've saved the world *and* I've got a tummy full of butterflies!"

"Yeah, no, you're not wrong. It isn't exactly something we can go around bragging about, though, since doing so would just be spreading the knowledge of what we were trying to save people from. It feels kind of weird to just celebrate it amongst ourselves."

"Don't introspect on it too much. It's still something we actually did, with our own six hands. There's fringe benefits to having done something awesome like that even if you can't put it on your CV."

"I did have a stand-off with an otherworldly demon for a couple minutes," I said, after a moment's consideration. "I guess standing up to Ian and booting him to the curb isn't so big of an obstacle after that."

"There ya go!"

"Is he still out there?"

"Probably. Want I should send him in?"

"Please."

Decca exited the room, shouted, "Yo Hollywood," and Ian entered shortly afterwards. He didn't look to be in much of a better state than I felt, and sat in the chair across from me with a heavy sigh. His feet stayed on the floor this time.

"So, Darren left his phone here when he went off after the fish things. I dunno if he's going to, like, come back here or what, but let him know I took it with me if he comes by looking for it."

It took me a second to realize he was referring to the person I'd only known as Lumberjack.

"Okay, sure, I'll make a note of that." I said. I grabbed a nearby pen and made a scribble on my desk calendar that looked something like the words 'Lumberjack phone.' "And now, and I'm honestly asking your input here, what are we to do about this project that's gotten a bit out of our hands?"

Ian grimaced. "Yeaaah, about that. I don't know that this

whole film thing can move forward after this. One of our cameras got stomped; I don't know what footage we had on that one. The other one is somewhere between here and wherever the fish guys went off to. I'll look at the footage when Darren gets back, but it's only like half of what we got. And any plans we had for filming in the gallery?" He gestured towards the door with an open hand.

"Look, I'm thankful that you helped us distract Tzmir and the Deep Guys and all that, but... you heard it back there. In the event that you do have any worthwhile shots, I don't think we want to disseminate anything about it, even under the guise of a cheap found footage movie."

"I'm right with you there, fuck a lot of that thing."

"But we've already announced that there's a film in the works. To street traffic, it very much looks like one hell of a film has been in the works for the last few days. Neither of us will look good if you don't deliver. What do we do here?"

Ian slouched back in the chair, pressing his fingers to his temples and scrunching up his face. Just when I thought he was only doing it sarcastically, he opened his eyes with a lightbulb-over-head expression.

"Distributors," he said.

"Pardon?"

"In a few months when people start asking, we tell them it's all tied up trying to find a distributor. Nobody wants to take a chance on such a bold project. Who knows if there's a market for it? Or maybe they're stuck in red tape negotiating rights with the owners of a store in the background of a shot whom we didn't get a release from. Legal mumbo-jumbo. You know how *those Hollywood types* are, am I right? There's plenty of ways it couldn't be our fault." He slid a hand palm-down across my desk. "That buck'll get passed."

I nodded, with a slow smile spreading across my face. For as much of a dick he was, he had at least a natural talent when it came to performative dickery, and could be goaded into using his talents for the benefit of society on occasion.

"Did we ever get around to signing whatever insurance waivers we were trying to before this all went to hell?" I said.

"I don't even remember, man; those were just some forms I got from OfficeMax anyways. Didn't even have them notarized."

To try and maintain the semblance of higher ground in the conversation, I didn't mention that I'd gotten my own grant contracts from probably the same aisle in the same store.

"Well, I'll see if I can't get your equipment covered in whatever sort of insurance I have to cover this place. It's the least I can do."

Ian shot me a finger-gun and clicked his tongue. "If anybody asks for the next couple weeks, say we're shooting off-site and refer 'em to me." He stood up, pushing off with both hands from the chair's arm rests. "As for the immediate future, I'm going off-site to take one bomb-ass nap and maybe see if Darren had any next of kin I might have to contact."

I wished him the best of luck with both endeavors and let him know I'd be in touch. Once he left, Decca swooped back in, taking the opportunity to prop her feet up on my desk, which I didn't mind so much. There didn't seem to be any blood spattered on them, and she kind of earned the right to do it.

"Board meeting," she said. "What's doing with the waify foundation now that Ian's out of the picture?"

"To all outside appearances, Ian is just doing a hell of a job shooting his movie and that's all we know about it. But behind the scenes, we'd seem to have an unexpected windfall to the exact amount we were planning to give him."

"So we can afford a lot of sushi meetings to work out how to do things on the level for next year."

"Oh God, no, never anything that might taste like those Deep Things smelled. But we're definitely not letting the situation get so desperate that we resort to either ancient monsters or a sequel to *Garden State*." I swallowed. In the physical sense, but there was also a good bit of pride along with it. "If you still want to be a part of the Withers Art & Inspiration Foundation, I have some serious fellowshipping opportunities for you."

"Part of me wants to say you've taken my help for granted before and almost wound up turning the Pioneer Valley into gibbering wrecks and making a Film Man was Not Meant to Screen at Sundance. Because you totally did that."

I nodded my head quite rapidly.

"But then again," she continued, "your phrasing makes it sound like I'll be fighting a horde of orcs. Do elaborate."

"I think it's become rather apparent that just because I have the resources doesn't mean I have the vision or vigor to do anything significant with it. And if I want to be a worthwhile wealthy benefactor instead of some sleazy media mogul, I should be self-aware enough to acknowledge that there are probably some better opinions about things than my own out there. Not just on ways to kill demon-squids, but... y'know. The social things you're always on about. So I guess I'm saying I'm in need of a creative director."

"You've got the right intentions, but whose got time to think," Decca asked with a lilt and a smile. She picked up her messenger bag and set it on my desk with its many sloganed pins facing me. "Fortunately, I've got a few ideas for you."

After Verrick got the painting installed with Myra's help, he came into my office and handed me two cards. One for Derby Solutions, whom he said were very discrete when it came to cleaning up Messes Man Was Not Meant to Spill, and one for your firm. He had nothing but positive things to say about your handling of his case against Voke & Quine Subsidiaries, and as you can probably tell, I'm rather at a loss as to how I might present this ordeal to a normal insurance company who probably don't deal with collateral squid-demon damage too often. I wouldn't know how to begin trying to argue that Old Ones count as deities for determining whether damage was caused by an Act of God. So I'd be extremely grateful for your firm's representation in this matter.

I can provide copies of what I think are the gallery's standard insurance policy as well as the forms that Ian had us sign. The damage to the premises occurred, to the best of my recollection, as described above. I apologize for the length of this letter, but it was a rather complicated set of circumstances and I've been told I get excessively wordy when nervous.

Sincerely,

Greg Withers
Chairman, Withers Art & Inspiration Foundation
(Decca is adamant that we get a better acronym.)

Acknowledgments

I'd like to thank the following people for helping this novel along, directly or otherwise:

Nate, Shaunn, and everybody else at Spaceboy Books who thought my wicked niche references were worth putting out there. Kyle Costaggini and Cassie Pruyn for keeping my excesses in check as beta readers. Amy Conner, Geoff Munsterman, Aimé SansSavant, Shadow Angelina Starkey, as well as several other writers/performers here in New Orleans who inspire and encourage me with their camaraderie. I'm honored to have shared stages, living room floors, backyards, and tacky booth seats with them.

About the Author

Zach Bartlett is a former Masshole living in New Orleans, where nobody ever listens to the Dropkick Murphys. His fiction has been published in magazines and podcasts, performed at three Fringe Festivals, and can often be heard at the spoken word series Esoterotica if you're ever in NOLA on a Wednesday. You can find more of his writing at http://zachbartlett.net, or watch him stick his foot in his mouth in real time as @zachbistall on Twitter.

About the Publishing Team

TJ Stambaugh received several commendations for his bravery as a battalion commander in the Meme Wars. TJ retired to Catonsville, MD, where he paints and enjoys movies you have to read. He's the founder and El Presidente of MoleHole Radio.

Shaunn Grulkowski has been compared to Warren Ellis and Phillip K. Dick and was once described as what a baby conceived by Kurt Vonnegut and Margaret Atwood would turn out to be. He's at least the fifth best Slavic-Latino-American sci-fi writer in the Baltimore metro area. He's the author of *Retcontinuum*, and the editor of *A Stalled Ox* and *The Goldfish*, all for 1888/Black Hill Press.